She flashed him a tentative smile.

'You should do that more often,' Cal murmured.

'I'm sorry?' Fran asked, confused.

'Smile. It makes you look so—so carefree, I suppose it is.'

Unsure if he was complimenting or criticising, Fran was relieved that they had arrived at the foot of the bed of Cal's next patient and she didn't have to answer.

Born in the industrial north, **Sheila Danton** trained as a Registered General Nurse in London, before joining the Air Force nursing service. Her career was interrupted by marriage, three children and a move to the West Country where she now lives. She soon returned to her chosen career, training and specialising in Occupational Health, with an interest in preventative medicine. Sheila has now taken early retirement, and is thrilled to be able to write full time.

Recent titles by the same author:

A GROWING TRUST

THE FAMILY TOUCH

BY
SHEILA DANTON

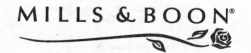

MILLS & BOON®

First published in Great Britain 1998
Harlequin Mills & Boon Limited,
Eton House, 18-24 Paradise Road, Richmond, Surrey TW9 1SR

© Sheila Danton 1998

ISBN 0 263 81420 3

Set in Times Roman 10 on 11¼ pt.
03-9902-53339-D

Printed and bound in Norway
by AIT Trondheim AS, Trondheim

CHAPTER ONE

FRAN BERGMONT ran her hands distractedly through her dark hair. Then she punched Dr Jenner's bleeper numbers into the telephone keypad for a third time.

The response this time was immediate. She snatched up the receiver and the moment he announced himself she snapped, 'Staff Nurse. D ward. You're needed here immediately.'

Without waiting for his response, she slammed the receiver back onto its cradle and raced back to Mrs Dubarry's room.

The young care assistant, sitting at the bedside, raised her eyes in unspoken query.

'He answered this time. I gave him no opportunity to argue.' Fran was already rechecking her patient's pulse and blood pressure.

When she'd finished she took one misshapen hand in hers and stroked the taut, dry skin, watching grimly as the life gradually ebbed from her patient's worn-out body.

'Do you want me to alert the crash team?' Allie asked anxiously.

Fran pointed to the highlighted message on the notes— NO RESUSCITATION.

When, some fifteen minutes later, Mrs Dubarry had lost all vital signs of life Fran tried to hide her fury at the continued non-appearance of Dr Jenner.

Having done all that was necessary for the moment, she silently indicated to her colleague that they should both move out of the small side ward.

'There's no family, is there?' the young girl whispered.

'No. The nursing home said there's no one.'

The plastic doors at the end of the ward corridor swung open as she spoke, admitting what seemed to be a whirl-wind in a white coat.

'You're too late, Dr Jenner,' Fran rebuked the youthful medic.

He shook his head, sending spikes of unruly blond hair in all directions. 'I'm Dr Ward—Rob. Just taken over from Dr Jenner for the night.'

Unfamiliar with the system of partial shifts worked by the house officers, Fran murmured apologetically. 'I...er... I see. We've been calling Dr Jenner to see a new admission for nearly an hour.'

Dr Ward sighed and held out his hands for the notes. 'I'll see her now.'

'She died ten minutes ago. We just need you to certify the fact.'

The young doctor frowned and made his way into the side ward. He soon emerged, and with a grimace muttered, 'She must have suffered hell with her arthritis.'

Fran nodded and led the way into the office. 'I presume that was one of the reasons why ''no resuscitation'' is marked on her notes. She couldn't have enjoyed much quality of life with that and her heart problems.'

'You say you've been calling the locum for an hour?' His steel-grey eyes searched her face relentlessly. 'He told me you'd only just rung as I walked in.'

Fran's jaw dropped in disbelief. 'Ask Allie, the care assistant. She tried a couple of times to reach him. We left messages everywhere.'

'So where did the ''no resuscitation'' tag come from?'

'A previous admission.'

She sensed his suspicion as he said, 'You're new to the department?'

'I've been on maternity leave,' she told him shortly, hoping he would read the anger in her dark eyes.

'I see.' He thumbed through the meagre notes hesitantly,

before lifting the receiver and dialling an internal number. 'I think the registrar should know about this.'

'You mean Dr Gunter?' Fran's relief at the thought of dealing with someone who knew her was short-lived.

'Dr Smith replaced him last month.'

Allie popped her head round the office door. 'Could you give me a hand to get Gladys back to bed?'

Fran nodded and followed Allie into the ward. After all, the living were much more important than post-mortems on the dead. Her thoughts, however, strayed repeatedly to the office as she wondered what the registrar was being told. Dr Ward was clearly ready to believe another doctor, rather than a nurse he didn't know.

It was nearly an hour before she and Allie had returned the more helpless patients to their beds, allowing Fran a chance to make her way back to the office to catch up on her paperwork.

She found Dr Ward in deep discussion with a dark-haired figure sitting opposite him. Although the newcomer had his back to Fran, his authority was evident from the set of his broad shoulders.

He turned at the interruption and Fran was stunned into silence as she was scrutinised by eyes of deepest blue. He rose to his feet to tower above even her own lofty height.

'You are the nurse in charge this evening?' His voice was deep, and he spoke with a soft, Gaelic rhythm that left his Scottish origin in no doubt.

Unprepared for the effect this incredibly good-looking male was having on her, Fran had to swallow hard before she could answer. 'Ye-es. I'm Staff Nurse Bergmont. Fran Bergmont.' Physically he was the exact opposite of his predecessor. Brian Gunter was a rounded, homely type who had put everyone at ease. The commanding presence of this new man, who was dressed in an expertly tailored light grey suit, suggested he could be very different.

She grasped the hand he extended in welcome, and when

their palms met his firm handshake triggered a shock wave that excited every nerve in her body. 'Pleased to meet you, Fran. I'm Callum Smith.'

As he released her hand she swallowed again, shaken by the first stirring of her emotions since Daniel had died. 'You replaced Dr Gunter?'

'Right.' His answering smile lit up not only his eyes but his whole face as he looked down at her with appreciation. 'I gather you've been on maternity leave.'

'You gather correctly.'

Although she smiled as she spoke, he must have noticed a shadow flit involuntarily across her face. 'I'm sorry. You had problems? The baby...?' His eyes held hers for longer than was necessary.

Fran shook her head. 'She's fine.'

He looked pointedly at her empty ring finger but, to her relief, didn't pursue the subject. Although it had been nearly a year since Daniel had died, she found well-meaning sympathisers the hardest to cope with.

'Dr Ward has been telling me of your problems with our locum earlier. Come and take the weight off your feet for a few moments. I'd like to hear your version of events.' The warmth of his invitation raised her hopes that he would at least listen to what she had to say, especially when he gave a nod of dismissal to the disbelieving young house officer.

Rob Ward took the hint immediately. 'I'll see if Allie needs anything, then check all's well across the way.'

As he closed the door behind him Dr Smith resumed his seat, completely at ease. Fran moved round to the office chair vacated by Dr Ward and, perching on the edge, waited for him to speak.

The registrar gestured towards the other armchair in the room. 'Take it easy, Fran. This isn't an inquisition.'

She moved, meeting his eyes with a challenge. 'I should

hope not. I believe I did all the right things. Even if Dr Ward doesn't.'

His eyes crinkled attractively as he shook his head. 'He didn't say that—only that neither you nor Dr Jenner were known to him personally—'

'And he preferred to take the word of a medic—'

'Why so defensive, Fran?'

He spoke quietly but incisively. Unable to read from his expression what he was thinking, she was acutely aware that he was someone she didn't want to think badly of her, and retorted, 'I'm not defensive, Dr Smith, but I've only been back at work two days and in that time I've worked with four different SHOs. I don't suppose they'd even remember my name, let alone vouch for my work.'

'Tell me about it.' He sighed wearily.

Fran murmured quietly, 'Apart from Allie, there's no one I remember still working in the unit.'

'It happens, but I believe it's no bad thing. Staff who remain in the same post for years tend to block innovative ideas. However, let's get back to Mrs Dubarry. Could earlier attention have saved her, do you think?'

Certain he was criticising her return to the unit, Fran shrugged. 'It's difficult to say, Dr Smith. Her heart failure was at an advanced stage. I'd say it was dehydration that killed her.'

Either ignoring or not recognising her terseness, he urged, 'If we're going to work together, drop the Dr Smith. I prefer Cal.'

When Fran didn't respond, he frowned pensively. 'Dr Jenner knew Mrs Dubarry's condition when he agreed to admit her from the nursing home?'

'I guess so, but I can't say for sure. All I received was a verbal message, telling me she was on her way.'

'From Dr Jenner?'

Embarrassed, Fran shook her head. 'It was someone he'd

asked to let me know. I presumed it was a nurse on another ward. We are so busy I'm afraid I didn't think to ask.'

Callum's answering smile was guarded. 'Thoughtless of me—I guess I'm delaying you unnecessarily. No doubt Dr Jenner has long since left the premises so I'll leave it until tomorrow to try and sort out what really happened. But I do recommend you make a careful note of all you did, including the times, in case there should be an inquiry.'

Sensing she was perhaps being naïve to trust him, Fran returned to the defensive. 'I've already done so roughly and intend to tidy my notes when I get a free moment. That won't be until I've handed over to the night staff.'

'That's late for you to be finishing, isn't it? Who's looking after your...er...daughter, wasn't it?'

Sure he didn't want the details, she murmured, 'She's in good hands.'

'Her father?' His interest surprised her.

'A child-minder, actually.' Sensing his disapproval, she added, 'Well, Jenny's more of a friend.'

'A friend?' he echoed. 'That must make it easier for you.'

Unsure what he was hinting at, she murmured, 'Yes. I'm happier, knowing she's with someone I can trust.'

'I can imagine.'

She experienced warm appreciation at his concern. Since Naomi's birth she'd become used to being the sole carer and having to make any decisions regarding her daughter.

Now, although they'd only just met, Callum's passing interest in her child's welfare made her realise just how lonely she had been. She would have liked to continue their chat, but it was impossible if she was to be ready to hand over to the night staff.

Callum appeared to read her mind. 'I won't keep you a moment longer, then.' He rose effortlessly from the depths of the armchair, oozing vitality as he did so.

As Fran watched him leave the office she experienced a

startling tinge of regret. He was someone she believed she could work with, but as she still had no idea how he felt about her handling of the earlier situation she wasn't at all sure he felt the same.

Her thoughts worked even harder while she and Allie toiled to settle the ward. From the few words they'd exchanged it had been obvious that Callum's patients would receive the latest thinking on care techniques. It was a pleasant surprise to find him working there, especially as Wenton wasn't exactly in the forefront of research or technology.

She was also surprised by the insistent memory of him, preventing her total concentration on her hand-over report. For the first time since Daniel's death she had to make a conscious effort to push thoughts of another man to the back of her mind. Even so, Cal obstinately refused to be ignored. To her dormant emotions he was a figure of fantasy.

The night nurse was another new face. 'Hi. I'm Michelle. How's things?'

Fran smiled a welcome. 'Not bad. With a bit of luck you should have a quietish night.' She ran through the report on each patient. 'I thought Mrs King might be a problem, but her blood pressure is fine at the moment. We had a death earlier and it upset her rather.'

'Who was that?'

'A new admission. Mrs Dubarry.'

'She's been in before, hasn't she?'

Fran nodded. 'So I believe. The care assistant remembered her, but no one else. The medical staff seem to change even more frequently than we do.'

'Too true. Apart from the reg. Have you met him yet? He's been with us a couple of months, I suppose. And is he dishy.'

'If you mean Dr Smith, I met him this evening for the first time.'

'He likes to be called Cal. He's made a real difference to the morale here. He's wonderful with the patients. He often pops in even when it's his day off and seems to really care about our working conditions. He sure is the most popular guy in the place.'

'He sounds too good to be true so, no doubt, he's already well and truly spoken for.' Although Fran spoke lightly, she had an irrational interest in the answer.

Michelle laughed and shook her head. 'He doesn't appear to be. That's why he's so popular! But you know these medics. He could have a wife, lurking somewhere, struggling on her own to bring up hordes of offspring. She probably wouldn't move if this is only a temporary post.'

Unwilling to let Michelle know that she, too, had been affected by the force of his magnetic personality, Fran nodded and joked. 'That figures. Good luck to him, then.' She handed over the drug keys. 'Hope it remains quiet for you. I've just a few notes to tidy up, then I'll be off. Have a good night.'

She settled at the desk to write her detailed account of Mrs Dubarry's admission and death. It took longer than she expected because she wanted to get the timing exactly right, so it was late when she eventually left the ward. As she ran to her car she couldn't help but wonder if returning to her old department had been such a good idea after all. Callum had hinted that he didn't approve of stick-in-the-muds!

But she'd always enjoyed working with geriatric patients, especially now so much could be done to rehabilitate them, so she'd decided a couple of years previously to concentrate on caring for them.

It wasn't a universally popular speciality. Consequently, the shortage of staff meant long and unsocial hours. Perhaps she ought to rethink. Maybe she would *have* to if her complaint about Dr Jenner wasn't believed.

She parked her car outside her child-minder's house and

rushed in to collect Naomi, who was contentedly asleep in Jenny's arms. A sudden burning jealousy rose in her throat, and for a moment she was tempted to snatch Naomi away and run with her as far from Jenny and Wenton as possible, never to return.

Then, recalling her need for an income and Cal's comment that she was fortunate to have someone she could trust to look after her daughter, she meekly thanked her. 'I'm sorry to be so late, Jen.' Aware how lucky she was that Jenny willingly accommodated the unsocial hours she worked, she continued, 'Hopefully, once I get back into the ward routine I'll finish earlier.'

'No problem. She's undressed and all ready for bed,' Jenny replied.

'Thanks a million for looking after her. We'd better go and give you a few hours' peace before we're back again. I'm on an early tomorrow.'

'I'll be here,' Jenny reassured her, as Fran wrapped Naomi snugly against the chill night air.

Fran secured her daughter in her car seat and, before climbing into the driver's seat, waved gratefully to her friend. Not for the first time, she offered a silent prayer that she had met Jenny when she had. Daniel had been such a caring person when he was alive, and she often wondered if he was still trying to make things easier for her.

'Motherhood is making you fanciful,' she admonished herself, aware that if she believed that she shouldn't be worrying quite so much about her unsettling shift at work.

She manoeuvred her car into the narrow drive of her cottage, and as she lifted her daughter from the car she thought about her meeting with Callum Smith and what Michelle had said about him. He'd certainly acquired a reputation throughout the hospital which she would be happy to endorse, but if he believed Dr Jenner's version of events he could well make trouble for her—and that was the last thing Fran needed.

She settled Naomi for the night and as she swiftly carried out a few necessary chores, before going to her own bed, her thoughts spun out of control, always with Callum Smith at the centre of them. Sometimes he was the understanding doctor she thought she had glimpsed, but more often someone who had the power to destroy her career.

When she finally switched off her bedside light, however, she was so exhausted that not even her racing thoughts could keep her awake.

The early news bulletin on her radio alarm woke her to the realisation that Naomi had slept through the night for the first time. Her morale boosted by a good night's sleep and the knowledge that the little girl clearly wasn't unsettled by the changes in her routine, Fran felt much happier at leaving her daughter with Jenny that morning.

'I'll be back about three to collect her.'

'She'll be here waiting when you come off duty.'

'You're a treasure, Jen. She even slept right through last night so she's obviously very happy with you. You've no idea how grateful I am.'

Jenny laughed. 'No more than I am that you allow me to look after her.'

Although she couldn't help wondering about the outcome of Callum probing into Mrs Dubarry's death, knowing her daughter was so contented lifted her spirits as she continued her journey to work. Until the events of the previous evening, she had felt she was settling comfortably back into her old routine, which boosted her confidence about her new responsibilities.

'Hi, Fran,' the night nurse greeted her. 'A couple of admissions overnight. One chronic asthmatic/bronchitic and one query heart failure, but all's peaceful this morning. Rob says he'll be down to brief you on what needs to be done before he goes off duty.'

'Fine. Who's taking over from him this morning?'

The night nurse shrugged. 'Should be the same locum as

last night, Dr Jenner, but apparently he hasn't put in an appearance as yet.'

Fran felt an optimistic flicker of relief at the news. If he couldn't be relied on to turn up on time for duty, perhaps she *would* be believed about his non-appearance the day before. However, that was something to deal with later. She didn't expect to see the registrar on the ward at this early hour.

Breakfast was being cleared away when Rob joined her at her desk. 'Did Dr Jenner say he'd be working today?'

Fran shrugged. 'I didn't meet him—and our exchanges on the telephone were brief in the extreme.'

'So you know next to nothing about him?'

Fran shook her head. 'I wouldn't recognize him if he walked through that door at this moment.'

He nodded. 'Of course! I remember. You thought I was him, didn't you?'

Fran nodded. 'You've been on call all this time?'

'Unfortunately. I'm bushed, but I'm still waiting to hand over to someone. If there's no locum I'll have to wait for Cal Smith to arrive.'

'Is there anything that needs to be done urgently?'

'Nothing that can't wait, but I'll tell you about the two new patients. Mrs Laker is in the early stages of heart failure and is very comfortable. I don't know why her GP admitted her as an emergency.' He handed her a drug chart. 'I've started her on these until Cal sees her.

'Mrs Jenkins is a chronic asthmatic and she was pretty ropey when she was admitted, but she's settling quite well.' He handed her another drug chart. 'If you've a moment, I'll introduce you to them both.'

When he'd done so, he said, 'The personnel department should be just about waking up so I'll go down and try to find out what's happening.'

It wasn't long before he returned. 'They wanted me to

stay on duty until lunchtime,' he told her, outraged. 'No way. The moment Cal shows his face I'm off.'

'I should think so, too. You must be dead on your feet already. I imagine Callum Smith is big enough to manage on his own for once.'

'Is that so?' Fran hadn't heard Cal coming along the corridor so his amused reaction to her comment sent colour flooding into her cheeks.

'I...er...' she mumbled, then added, 'Good morning, Dr Smith.'

He lifted an eyebrow in surprise. 'I thought we'd progressed to Cal.'

'Yes, sorry, I wasn't expecting you yet.'

'I can believe that, after hearing you encouraging Rob to desert his post.'

'He *has* been on duty for the last twelve hours plus.' Fran defended herself hotly.

Cal was clearly amused. 'In that case, the sooner he tells us what's happening and gets off to his bed the better. Who's taken over from you this morning, Rob?'

'No one at the moment.'

Callum raised his eyes to the heavens. 'Any reason?'

'Apparently, Dr Jenner was booked but hasn't shown up or telephoned to say why.'

Fran could see the registrar was far from happy at the news. 'You'd better tell me the important details, then.'

'The only real problem is with one of the new admissions, Mrs Jenkins. She's a chronic asthmatic and lives alone, which obviously doesn't help when she has an attack. Fran has her drug charts and all the other gen. So, if it's OK with you, I'm off to bed.'

'With Fran so concerned about your welfare, I wouldn't dare object,' he teased.

'I'd feel the same about any SHO who'd worked for the last twelve hours,' she retorted indignantly.

'But you think registrars are big enough to take care of themselves,' Callum bantered.

'I didn't say that!' She tried to will herself not to blush, but it didn't work, and she turned away to avoid his gaze. 'I must go and check on Mrs Jenkins again,' she murmured, before moving hastily towards the ward.

'Let me know if there's a problem.' The amusement Fran heard in his voice told her he knew she was escaping from his badinage. 'If not,' he added, 'when I've had a quick chat with Rob I'll go down to Medical Personnel and see what's being done about a replacement doctor.'

Fran nodded. She checked all was well with her patients then despatched the care assistant for a quick coffee break, before starting on those tasks she could deal with herself.

Callum Smith soon re-appeared, but it was quite some time after Fran had noticed him go into the ward office that he came in search of her. 'I know you're busy, but when you have a few spare moments I'd like to see you in the office.'

'I'll just finish this dressing and I'll be with you.'

He nodded agreeably.

Mrs Ashton, whose varicose ulcer Fran was dressing, grinned. Her eyes alight with amusement, she said, 'I wish he wanted to see me alone in the office. He's the goods and no argument.'

Fran knew she was blushing. 'You mustn't say things like that. He's probably a married man.'

'I shouldn't think that'll bother him when he's with someone as pretty as you.'

Fran never ceased to be amazed by the outrageous comments of her patients, especially the older ones. They appeared to throw away their inhibitions when they were admitted to hospital.

'You'd better not let him hear you say that,' she joked. 'He'll throw you out if he does and then who'll do your dressing?'

Mrs Ashton's answer was a chuckle.

'Nearly done now. Just as well, before you say anything more.'

As Fran finished her task her thoughts focused automatically on the events of the previous evening so that by the time she joined Cal she was anxious about the reason for his summons. The warmth of his welcome, however, swept away her fears.

'Take the weight off your feet for a few moments, Fran.'

'They could certainly do with a rest, but I can only stay a moment. I do need to keep an eye on Mrs Jenkins.'

When she had done as he'd suggested, he continued, 'You haven't stopped all morning. Haven't you any help?'

'Only a care assistant from the agency. She doesn't know the routine or the patients.'

'Where's Allie?'

'She started a week's leave today.'

'That's bad timing.' He handed her a cup of coffee from the machine which was steaming on the window-sill. 'So, how's our unit's latest recruit this morning?'

'Busy,' Fran told him, as she started to bring the patients' care records up to date, 'but enjoying it.'

Callum settled back into his comfortable chair but Fran, still apprehensive, couldn't relax. She raised her eyes to search his face, wanting to know what he was really thinking. Her eyes were caught and held by his, and she was startled by the compassion she again saw there.

'Did you have a disturbed night with your daughter?'

She shook her head, then stammered, 'Just the opposite. She slept right through for the first time.'

He nodded, but was clearly only partially satisfied. 'So what kept you awake?'

She shrugged. 'Nothing. I slept well. When I eventually got to bed. I—I suppose it'll take me a little time to get back into a working routine again. I've had it easy for the last six months.'

He shook his head, and his smiling gaze searched her face relentlessly. 'You have to be up early with your little girl?'

Fran shrugged. 'I'm used to it.'

'But not when you've worked late the evening before?'

She sighed and shrugged but, unsure where his probing was leading, she didn't speak. If he wasn't going to raise the subject of Mrs Dubarry's death, neither was she.

'Any worries?'

Believing he must have read her mind, Fran gave a startled gasp before she realised he was talking about the patients. Hoping he hadn't noticed her gaffe, she shook her head. 'As Rob told you, he'd already dealt with my queries.'

'I wish we could find a few more like him to join our team. Wenton doesn't attract the kind of doctors we need.'

'What made you move here?'

'I was Pam Wood's senior house officer in Essex when she was a registrar. She begged me to come and support her. She's a brilliant geriatrician and I hope to learn a lot from her.'

'The patients sing your praises. They don't think you need to learn anything.'

'That's because Mrs Wood is kept busy on the male side at the moment. She has no registrar there and so leaves the ladies to me.'

Although she had to admit she was enjoying the rapport between them, she drained her coffee-cup, replaced it on the desk, and murmured, 'I can't sit here all morning—I've too much to do.'

'Your dedication to your patients does you credit, but surely your daughter needs you just as much. Wouldn't part-time work suit you better?'

Wouldn't it just? But life wasn't so easy. His words had stayed her hand as she'd been about to pull open the office door. Was this his way of telling her the powers that be thought she hadn't coped the previous evening? Or was it just that he didn't trust her with his patients?

'It's a bit early to start making changes. I haven't worked a full week as yet,' she protested, tugging open the door. 'I must get on.'

'Can we do a ward round now?'

Fran nodded. 'Whenever you like,' she told him stonily.

Once again he appeared to read her mind. 'You're not worrying about last night, are you? Even if questions are asked, if you know you did your best, you have nothing to fear.'

'Apart from Rob believing Dr Jenner's version of events rather than mine.'

'That was just initially,' he murmured. 'You can't have failed to notice that he hasn't a bad word to say for you today. But I don't need to tell you that, do I?' he persisted. 'You and Dr Ward are obviously good friends now.'

Fran felt a perverse satisfaction that Callum didn't appear best pleased by the fact. Her confidence rose steeply as she prepared the notes trolley for the ward round.

Let him think what he liked. She wouldn't give him the satisfaction of a reply.

'You seemed to be getting on exceptionally well to me.' Fran glanced up at him as he spoke and surprised a look of near disapproval on his face. Surely he ought to be pleased that she and his one permanent colleague were working well together. Shouldn't he?

CHAPTER TWO

As FRAN started to open the office door again, her composure rattled by Cal returning to the subject. 'Before we start this round tell me just one more thing. Did Dr Jenner seem at all agitated when you saw him yesterday?'

'I never saw him. He approved everything verbally and said he'd be down later to sign for them. Bring the notes up to date, in other words.'

'And he didn't.'

'No,' she answered more vehemently than she'd intended. 'I never met the man. He didn't come near the place all afternoon or evening. I—'

'Did you administer any drugs not signed for?' he broke in sharply.

Fran shook her head and sighed deeply. 'I *do* know better than to do that. I—'

'So what *did* he authorise?'

'I told him about the changes in the condition of various patients and suggested tests and observations that might be helpful. I didn't think about it at the time, but he agreed with everything I suggested. I always made my own notes about it and stated what time I'd informed him of the changes and his response.'

Callum nodded. 'Did it seem to you that he was avoiding making a decision?'

'You mean—w-was he bogus?' Fran stammered.

Callum shook his head. 'He doesn't seem to have been. Medical Personnel have checked and can find nothing wrong with his CV.'

Fran chewed anxiously at her bottom lip. 'So what's going to happen?'

21

'There'll be a post-mortem on Mrs Dubarry. Any decision will be made after that. I imagine that Dr Jenner will not be employed here again.'

Fran offered a silent prayer of gratitude, before saying, 'Right, let's see what's happening with the living patients. These first two on the left are the night's admissions. Mrs Jenkins is the asthmatic admitted in the early hours—Rob appears to have her reasonably stabilised.'

'Hello, Mrs Jenkins. I'm Dr Smith, the registrar.' He studied the charts at the end of her bed. 'You've had a bit of a torrid night, haven't you?'

His deep voice soothed with every syllable and Fran watched the over-anxious patient relax.

Cal seated himself by the side of the bed and took the patient's hand. 'Judging by your notes, this is a fairly frequent occurrence. You live alone, don't you?'

Mrs Jenkins nodded, and Fran could see tears at the back of her eyes. 'My husband died a couple of years ago.'

Cal nodded and made a few notes. 'We'll keep you in for now and set up a few tests. See if we can't do something to make your breathing a bit easier.'

As they moved away from the bed he murmured to Fran, 'She needs to know there's someone around, otherwise she panics—and this is the result. She'd be much better in warden-controlled accommodation, somewhere where she can be independent but know there's help at hand. I think we'd see less of her in here then.'

Fran nodded. 'I couldn't agree more, but sheltered housing is in short supply.'

He nodded his acknowledgement, but as they'd reached the bedside of the next admission he said no more. 'Well, Mrs Laker, we meet again. Remember me? Dr Smith? We met in Outpatients last week.'

The patient smiled up at him, obviously as smitten as everyone seemed to be who came into contact with him. 'The doctor last night gave me some different tablets.'

When he had listened to her chest and checked her prescription sheet, Cal nodded approvingly. 'Good. Dr Ward's done exactly what I would have done. I'll be back later to see how the change in treatment is working.'

He smiled ruefully at Fran as his bleeper went off. 'I'll go and see what's wanted. In the meantime, perhaps you could arrange for her to have a chest X-ray.'

He was soon back. 'Mrs Wood is on C ward so I want to update her on what's been happening. I'll be back as soon as I can to finish the round.'

Fran watched anxiously as he left the ward. She hadn't met the consultant as yet and hated to think that what Cal had to tell her might give her a wrong impression.

He returned much sooner than she'd expected. Fran was in the treatment room, preparing for another dressing, when she heard his voice behind her.

'Shall we finish the ward round now?'

'I wasn't expecting you yet. Was Mrs Wood busy?'

He frowned. 'I spoke to her briefly, but told her that I didn't want to delay you any longer than necessary. You have enough to do before you get back to your daughter.'

Fran drew in a deep breath. Had she misread what he'd meant earlier? Had his suggestion about shorter hours been purely for Naomi's benefit?

It was the last thing she would have expected, but it was certainly a warming thought. She flashed him a tentative smile, before leading the way into the ward.

'You should do that more often,' he murmured.

'I'm sorry?'

'Smile. It makes you look so—so carefree, I suppose it is.'

Unsure if he was complimenting or criticising, she was relieved that they had arrived at the foot of the bed of his next patient and she didn't have to answer.

'Mrs Fenner's blood sugar is stabilising *and* she's lost

nearly half a stone,' she told him as he greeted the over-weight occupant of an armchair in the corner.

'And that's still on diet alone?'

At Fran's nod he continued, 'That's good news. And how are you enjoying the food we're giving you?' He perched himself on the arm of Mrs Fenner's chair.

'S'alright, I suppose. I gets hungry sometimes, though.'

He rested a consoling hand over hers. 'Give your body time to adapt. It's early days yet.'

'G'arn with you,' she said with a laugh. 'You told me that last week and I ain't noticed no difference.'

He chuckled. 'You'll think it worth it when that husband of yours has to buy you a new outfit!'

The genial Mrs Fenner laughed uproariously at his comment. 'I doubt if I'll live to see that day, luv.'

Callum rose to his feet as he said to her, 'It could be sooner than you think. I see no reason why you shouldn't go home soon and attend the diabetic clinic each week.'

'My Sid *will* be pleased. He's useless, looking after himself.'

As they moved away he said to Fran, 'Before we let her go get the dietician to reinforce all she's been told already—when her husband's there if possible. Compliance is nearly always improved by an understanding partner.'

For a moment she thought he sounded discouraged. 'You obviously don't think Sid is one.'

'It wasn't him I was thinking about,' he told her absently, before apparently dismissing the thought and moving on towards the next patient.

To hide her curiosity as to whom exactly he was thinking about, she bent her head to make a few notes to remind herself of what needed to be done.

'Mrs Fenner *is* on a maintenance dose of aspirin, isn't she?'

When Fran didn't reply immediately he explained, 'Low

doses are now thought to stop some of the complications of diabetes setting in.'

Fran nodded, 'I know. I was just checking that she has been prescribed them—and she has.'

'Right. Good morning, Mrs Laing. How are you today?' He had stopped beside a wiry, grey-haired lady whose fingers were plucking restlessly at the blanket covering her knees.

Startled by his voice, she gave him a half-smile, before saying coquettishly, 'Better for seeing you, Dr Smith.'

'What are you after today?' he teased, taking her hand in his to check on her pulse rate.

'To see the television. It's just starting.'

'What is?' Fran queried.

'The morning magazine programme. That presenter. He's just like Dr Smith. Handsome. That's what he is.'

Fran murmured quietly, 'If you'll excuse me, I'll just walk her down to the day room.'

Laughing, he shook his head. 'I'll do it. It's not every day I receive such an extravagant compliment.' He lifted the blanket from the elderly lady's knee and helped her to her feet.

His whole attention was tuned in to what she was saying as they walked down the ward, and Fran watched Mrs Laing blossom and open up to him. The force of his charm was encouraging her to chat to him in a way Fran hadn't seen her do with anyone else. He certainly had as winning a way with his patients as with his colleagues. She really shouldn't be surprised at his concern for her and her daughter's welfare. It was the way he was.

On his return they moved on towards the next patient, Miss George. When she had been admitted the previous morning, Callum had suspected inflammation of the arteries in her head.

She had dismissed her increasing stiffness as being due to age until the previous day when she'd developed unbearable pains in her head and face and her GP had requested hospital admission.

Cal had started her on a high dose of steroids.

'How's the headache today?' he asked her.

She smiled up at him as if he were a god.

'Much, much better. You're a magician.'

He smiled. 'Not me. It's the steroid tablets we're giving you.'

'Whatever, I can't thank you enough. I never want to go through that again.'

'I hope you won't have to. Hopefully, a biopsy will confirm our diagnosis then we can start reducing the dosage to a level which won't cause any side-effects but will keep the pain at bay.'

'How long will I have to take them?'

'It varies. It could be between one and two years, maybe longer. Your doctor mentioned that recently you've had problems, doing simple tasks, because of stiffness.'

'That's right...'

'Any less stiff this morning?'

Miss George thought about her answer. 'I haven't tried to do anything but get out of bed but, come to think of it, that was easier than it has been.'

'That's as a result of the steroid tablets as well.'

'That's incredible. If I can do things for myself again it was worth suffering that headache.'

'I'm pleased to hear it. I'm going to ask another doctor to take over your care. He specialises in rheumatic diseases of which we're pretty sure this is one.'

When they returned to the office he rang the hospital rheumatologist. 'I think we have as clear-cut a case of polymyalgia rheumatica, complicated by arteritis, as you'll ever see. Her name's Miss George and the condition is already responding to steroids.'

He replaced the receiver and grinned ruefully at Fran.

'I've just given my most grateful patient away. Fancy being called a magician!'

Fran said, 'They might not say it but most of them think it. You certainly made Mrs Laing's day. I've never seen her so animated as when you escorted her to the day room.'

He shrugged. 'I wanted to check how steady she is on her pins and at the same time assess her mental state. I was very impressed. We'll be able to discharge her soon.'

When he'd gone Fran did a quick drug round and then helped her care assistant to get several more of the patients into chairs and made up a few beds. She couldn't believe it when she saw the patients' lunches waiting to be served.

It wasn't a task to be rushed, and by the time the dishes were cleared away she had no time for lunch herself. She had too much paperwork to catch up on.

It was time for the afternoon shift to relieve her before she realised it, and the moment she saw them her thoughts turned to Naomi. The thought of spending a quiet evening at home with her was magical.

As she settled her daughter later that evening she thought about Cal, who clearly wanted his patients to have nothing but the best of care. His comments earlier in the day still rankled with Fran, making her wonder if her working hours *were* too long.

By the next morning she had come to the conclusion that they weren't. She enjoyed her work. Most of the time. And as Naomi grew up she would need space. The last thing she would need was a doting mother, with nothing but her daughter to think about.

She also discounted her niggling worry that Cal might not trust her with his patients. It was so unlikely it was laughable. She had allowed the events of Tuesday evening to assume gigantic proportions because it was her first week back at work. She would probably not hear another word about it.

Relieved not to have to scrape the windscreen free of ice

for once, she set out in plenty of time for her late shift and felt almost content when she handed Naomi over to Jenny and made her way onto the geriatric ward to concentrate on the hand-over report.

'Who's the houseman today?' she asked tentatively, before Kelly left her to it.

'Another new locum. Gerald. He seems an improvement on some we've had recently. At least Cal seems to be happy to trust him to get on with things.'

Fran nodded, 'I'm glad to hear it.'

Kelly looked at her with wide eyes. 'Of course, you were on duty when...' She stopped, unsure how to finish what she'd been about to say.

'When Mrs Dubarry was admitted. Yes, I'm afraid so.'

'Oh, well, the dust seems to be settling now, doesn't it?'

'The dust? You mean—?'

'Only that nothing's been said for a couple of days,' Kelly broke in hurriedly. 'I'm off now. See you tomorrow.'

Fran watched her leave the office with a momentary sense of unease. What dust had Kelly been talking about? Telling herself that the girl was probably an inveterate gossip who loved to exaggerate, Fran shrugged and got on with her work.

Cal came onto the ward as she was helping Mrs Laing down to the day room. When Fran acknowledged his presence he indicated he would wait for her in the office.

When she joined him he welcomed her warmly and, rising to his feet, asked, 'Can we go and look at Mrs Jenkins? She's not doing too well.'

Having hoped for a moment's respite for her feet, she gave a resigned nod, but the moment she moved towards the door he grasped her arm. 'Is something troubling you, Fran?'

'Nothing. It's just—nothing, really. I'm still not sure about the ward routine, that's all.'

She knew he didn't believe her, but she shook her arm

free and, lifting a batch of notes from the desk, made her way quickly into the corridor before he could say so.

As they made their way to the furthermost bed she sensed him watching her, and when she turned to meet his eyes the tender expression she saw there caused the muscles of her chest to clench painfully.

Trying to ignore the effect his solicitude was having on her, she placed her notes on Mrs Jenkins's locker and drew the curtains round the bed space. 'Dr Smith has come to see what you're up to now you're out of sight.'

Cal warmed his stethoscope in his hand. 'Let's have a listen to your chest.'

Fran assisted him with a thorough examination of his patient, during which their hands brushed frequently, exciting the nerve endings in her skin. It was like delicious torture by the time he nodded reassuringly to the patient. 'Better than when I last listened in.'

Mrs Jenkins looked up at him anxiously. 'Will I be going home?'

'Not yet.' He pointed to the empty bed next to her. 'It's a bit isolated down here, though. Wouldn't you rather be nearer the action?'

'I suppose I can always go to the day room if I want company,' she responded doubtfully.

'Hmm. I'll see if I can find a friendly neighbour for you.'

He patted his patient's hand and set off back down the ward. When they reached the office he turned to Fran angrily. 'She should have access to oxygen at all times. Why on earth was she moved so far down?'

'To stop her worrying about her condition, I guess.' Fran didn't know who had made the decision, but tried to defend them. 'You wouldn't believe the ideas these patients have. Those in the first couple of bed spaces are known to be there for us to keep an eye on, and Mrs Jenkins was probably thinking it meant we weren't expecting her to get better.'

'Well, I'm afraid she'll have to move back but, obviously, not to the top. Which is the last bed space with piped oxygen?'

'Four.'

He looked up the ward. 'If we move her to that one we can just shunt all the rest down one.' He turned to look at Fran. 'But I don't want you doing it.'

'I can manage.'

'You're not moving her on your own. I'll call Gerald and it won't take a moment.'

'I can ring for the porters.'

'No need.' He laughed. 'If Gerald and I do it we can make sure that Mrs J. doesn't think about the reasons for the move. I guarantee it.' He lifted the receiver and summoned Gerald to the ward.

As Fran watched them, laughing and joking with their patients, Cal rose even higher in her esteem. Nothing was too much trouble for him.

He really was a registrar in a million. He'd anticipated any anxiety over the move by suggesting they were moving Mrs Jenkins for her benefit rather than for her health. And he was so cheerful. It was no wonder he could do nothing wrong in the patients' eyes—or the staff's, for that matter.

She rewarded them with a tray of tea when they eventually returned to the office. 'Thanks for doing that.'

Cal acknowledged her thanks with a smile. 'I enjoyed myself. I had a holiday job as a hospital porter when I was at med school. I found a lot more out about my patients in those days than I do now when I try to discover their medical history!'

Fran didn't pour herself a cup of tea, and was preparing to leave the office when Cal enquired, 'Where are you off to?'

'I've got a hundred and one things to do, including a drug round. Why? Was there something else you wanted to discuss?'

Cal shook his head. 'No, but you deserve a cuppa as well.'

Fran shook her head. 'No time. I'll get one when I've a spare moment.'

When she returned to the office some time later Cal was still there. 'Have you had supper?'

She shook her head. 'I'll eat when I get home.'

'Someone will have it ready for you?'

She knew he was probing about her domestic arrangements and decided to give him the bare facts but nothing more.

'Apart from Naomi, I live alone. I'm sorry, Cal. I must get on now.'

He watched her pensively, but didn't attempt to detain her. She didn't see him for the remainder of her shift or for most of her late shift on Friday, and she wondered if it was her own fault. Perhaps she should have been a bit more forthcoming about her living arrangements, but she hated talking about Daniel's death. And that's where their conversation would inevitably have led.

She was discussing the problem of Mrs Jenkins's sheltered housing with Gerald when Cal appeared in the office doorway. 'Hi. Everything OK?'

They both nodded and Fran felt she had to say something. 'I'm just waiting to hand over to the night shift.'

Cal pulled a chair towards him and straddled it the wrong way. 'Before you go, Fran, there is something I've been meaning to ask you. Will you be able to organise a baby-sitter for the firm dinner next Friday?'

Fran looked at Gerald and back to Cal. 'The firm dinner? Surely that's just for medical staff. I won't be invited.'

'I think you'll find you will. Our esteemed consultant is very forward thinking, and she has been very impressed with what she's heard of your work this week.'

'But—'

'Mrs Wood likes the nurses in charge to join our get-togethers. She considers we should be a team, all pulling in the same direction. Not easy with the shortage of staff as it is at the moment, but someone of your capabilities will go a long way to making up for that.'

'Nice of you to say so,' Fran joked nervously.

'Not my words. Mrs Wood's. Perhaps your friend Jenny would help you out on Friday. It would be useful if you could join us.'

'I'll ask her. *If* I'm invited.'

'You will be,' he told her with certainty. 'And you'll enjoy it. She does all the catering herself.'

Fran was thoughtful as she left the hospital. She'd still not met Mrs Wood, the consultant, because she was more often on the male side of the unit. Fran found it difficult to believe she would issue an invitation to someone she didn't know.

Unless Cal had pressurised her to do so, perhaps as a result of her telling him that she lived alone. The thought sent a surprising shiver of excitement scudding down her spine. However, when she collected Naomi that evening she didn't mention the babysitting to Jenny. That way she wouldn't look a fool if the invitation didn't materialise.

When she'd placed Naomi securely in her car seat she settled herself behind the steering-wheel. It wasn't until she was belted up that she noticed a piece of paper secured under the windscreen-wiper.

Roundly cursing the advertiser who was causing one more delay in a tiring day, she climbed out into the bitter wind and snatched it up, angrily crumpling the paper.

Her name, printed in bold red letters, caught her eye. 'What on earth...?'

She unfolded the note, and what she read drained the colour from her cheeks. 'If you know what's good for you and your daughter, keep your mouth shut about Dr Jenner.'

Puzzled, she screwed up the note and threw it into a rubbish bag in her car. Was this someone having a joke with her? She knew nothing about the man, apart from him not answering her repeated calls. Nothing more had been said about the events of that evening so why would anyone bother to search out her car at Jenny's house and leave such a dramatic note?

She shrugged, and although she tried to dismiss the note as a stupid prank an icy chill clutched at her heart. When she tried to drive away her shaking limbs refused to co-operate immediately and she drove home much more slowly than usual.

By the time she'd settled Naomi and had had a leisurely cup of coffee, she tried to laugh at herself, but it wasn't easy and she was so tired that she didn't bother with any food.

Her unsettled frame of mind, combined with her empty stomach, meant she spent a restless night. Consequently, she overslept on Saturday morning and had to skip breakfast to get Naomi to Jenny and on to the unit on time.

The Saturday morning shift seemed more arduous than usual and she knew it was because she was tired, and more than a little frightened. And as Mrs Wood had insisted Cal take the weekend off, there was no one to share her coffee break. So she didn't bother.

She missed lunch so that she would be ready to leave on time. 'I'm sorry we're disrupting your weekend like this,' she told Jenny when she arrived to collect Naomi.

'You worry too much,' Jenny told her. 'You know looking after her is as much for my benefit as for yours. I'll tell you what. I thought I'd go to an antique-cum-bric-à-brac fair at the town hall. Why don't you come with me? We could have tea there. I'm sure you'd enjoy that.'

Fran nodded. 'I would. I haven't done anything but work this week.'

'I know. You look worn out and I'm sure you're losing weight. You get Naomi ready while I lock up. And we'll have a wickedly delicious cream tea.'

Fran could think of nothing more welcome. She was starving. 'It'll be easier to take my car for Naomi.'

It was only a short journey, and Fran found a place to park right outside the hall. She lifted Naomi's buggy from the car boot and, having strapped her in, they made their way into the fair.

The hall was crowded and it wasn't long before the airless heat combined with her empty stomach to make Fran feel queasy. She tried to ignore it by leaning a little more heavily on the buggy handles.

Jenny hadn't noticed anything amiss. She was enthusing over a couple of brass bells. One was in the form of a lady in a crinoline. 'I'd love these for my collection. Hang on a minute while I push my way through and do a bit of bargaining.'

Fran looked around her, but there was nowhere to sit. She moved on to the next stall to try and forget her discomfort.

Naomi woke and, raising her arm, knocked her teddy out of the buggy. Taking a deep breath, Fran bent to pick it up. As she reached out for it everything went black momentarily.

'Move back, give her some air,' she heard as she tried to struggle to her feet. She felt herself being gently pushed down again as a familiar masculine scent assailed her nostrils and a voice she recognised only too well murmured to those still around her, 'I'm a doctor. I'll look after her.'

Fran struggled to sit up, and Cal placed an arm around her shoulders to support her. 'As soon as you feel like it, we'll get you out into the fresh air. It's unbearably hot in here.'

Jenny was beside them now, looking worried. 'I'll take Naomi, Fran. Don't you worry about her.'

Her head swimming, Fran tried to protest, but the words she sought weren't there. Instead she managed, 'Thanks, Jenny.'

Cal smiled approvingly. 'Pleased to meet you, Jenny. I've heard about you.'

She looked puzzled. 'You know Fran?'

'We work together.' He helped Fran to her feet. 'We'll be just outside.'

He led her through the crowded hall and outside to a bench seat in the town-hall gardens.

'Better?' he asked as he seated himself beside her.

She nodded and then wished she hadn't as another wave of nausea swept over her. She took several deep breaths and he took hold of her wrist to check her pulse.

'When did you last eat?' he asked her suspiciously.

'I—I don't remember.'

'Did you have lunch?'

'There wasn't time.'

'What did you have for breakfast?'

When she didn't answer he sighed accusingly. 'Have you eaten at all today?'

'I had a cup of coffee.'

'The pub across the road does meals all day. I'll just let Jenny know where we'll be.'

'Ask her to join us. We were going to treat ourselves to tea at the fair.'

He nodded.

He was soon back and, grasping her arm, he raised her tenderly to her feet. His touch heated her skin and her knees buckled beneath her.

When she'd recovered he led her to a table in the window of the Hare and Rabbit.

'Would you like a brandy to revive you?'

'No, thanks. I'm driving.' Feeling more than a little foolish, she looked around her anxiously. 'Is Jenny coming?'

'Later. She'll join us for coffee.'

Fran tried to make sense of what Cal was saying. 'But—but we were going to have a cream tea.'

'Don't worry about her. She's having a great time, searching through boxes and boxes of junk.'

'What about Naomi?'

'She's happily watching. Completely unfazed. Now, what would you like to eat?'

'Are you eating?'

Exasperated, he thrust the menu towards her. 'Stop worrying about other people for once. *You* need to eat and that's all that matters.'

She turned her attention to the menu and chose the first thing her eyes alighted on. 'The vegetable lasagna will be fine.'

'What to drink?'

'Sparkling mineral water, please.'

She relaxed back into the window-seat and watched him as he gave his order. He was incredibly confident in everything he did, and she was grateful to him for taking control. He returned to the table with her water and a glass of red wine for himself.

She took a sip of the bubbling water gratefully.

'Better?'

She nodded.

He scrutinised her face closely. 'You don't look as if you slept much last night.'

What was he insinuating? That she'd been out, enjoying herself? 'I'm just tired, not yet used to trying to juggle work and looking after Naomi.'

He must have sensed her resentment. He grinned widely and said, 'I wasn't suggesting you were painting the town red. Far from it. You know, I admire your dedication to work and childcare, but you do need some time to yourself as well.'

'I have plenty of that when Naomi is sleeping.'

'But do you allocate a proportion of your time to something you enjoy?'

'I'm here at the antiques fair today, aren't I?'

He regarded her steadily for a long moment. 'You're only here because Jenny suggested it.'

'I—I—'

'You may as well admit it because she told me so. She thought the outing would do you good. She's over there, filled with remorse at dragging you along.'

Fran shrugged defensively, but she was saved from answering by the arrival of her lasagna, together with a toasted sandwich for Cal. Relieved that she didn't have to respond, or eat alone, she tucked in hungrily to the piping-hot food.

When she'd finished she leaned back on the settle and said gratefully, 'That was delicious.'

'Would you like a dessert?'

'I couldn't eat another thing.'

'Coffee?'

'In a minute. When Jenny joins us.'

He watched her thoughtfully, then said, 'Before she does, there are a few questions I'd like answered.'

'Such as?' Fran fidgeted nervously.

'Jenny told me Naomi's father is dead.'

'So?'

'I'd like to hear about it,' he said gently, 'from you.'

CHAPTER THREE

FRAN inhaled deeply. She knew she would have to explain some time but she had wanted to do it in her own time and in a way that didn't beg Cal's sympathy. 'Naomi's father worked for an aid agency. He knew it was risky and his luck ran out. Daniel had made some provision but, both for my sanity and those little luxuries like food, I needed to return to work.'

He frowned at her cynical response. 'I'm sorry. I shouldn't have asked.'

'No. It's me who should apologise. It's my way of dealing with the painful memories.' She swallowed hard to prevent tears spilling over onto her cheeks.

He rested a hand gently over hers. 'I'd like to hear the whole story some time. But not now. I think we could do with our coffee.'

Fran struggled to control her voice before she spoke, 'I thought we were waiting for Jenny to join us.'

Cal nodded towards the window he was facing. 'She's crossing the road at this very moment.' He moved to the bar to put in the order.

Jenny joined her at the table with Naomi asleep again in the buggy. 'You look better,' she greeted Fran as she settled in the seat Cal had vacated.

Aware that an improved state of health wasn't the reason for the heightened colour Jenny had noted in her cheeks, Fran said, 'It was food I needed. Cal's just gone to get coffee. Would *you* like something to eat?'

'Coffee's fine. Look what I've found.' She excitedly unwrapped a selection of bells. 'You must have brought me luck.'

Fran murmured her admiration, before whispering to Jenny, 'What have you been saying about me?'

Her friend frowned. 'Telling Cal, you mean?'

'Telling Cal what?' He seated himself beside Fran on the cushioned settle.

'Oh, er, we were just talking about these bells.' Fran hastily changed the subject.

Cal admired Jenny's finds, but as the coffee arrived the sideways glance he gave Fran told her he hadn't believed her and she regretted her curiosity.

'As soon as we've finished these I must get Naomi home, if that's OK by you, Jenny.'

'No problem. I've spent all I can afford.'

'Are you sure?' Cal asked. 'I can drive you home later if you want to go on rummaging at the sale.'

Suspicious that Cal wanted to question Jenny further about her, Fran held her breath until Jenny refused the offer. 'I've seen all I want to, thanks. Brian will be back from the football by now, and wondering where I am.'

'Thanks for the food and for looking after me,' Fran murmured as they left the pub together. 'I'll see you on Monday, Cal.'

'If not before.'

'I wonder what he meant by that?' she asked Jenny, as she settled Naomi into her car seat.

'He's lovely, Fran. You never let on you were working with a Celtic god!'

Fran laughed dismissively. 'He's a very good doctor.'

'He certainly looked after you this afternoon.'

'Probably just making sure I won't let him down by going sick!'

'That's cruel, Fran.' Jenny laughed as Fran brought the car to a stop outside her house. 'He looked really concerned about you. See you early tomorrow, then?'

'I'm afraid so. Brian's good to put up with all these early mornings.'

'He's as fond of Naomi as I am, Fran, and, although he wasn't convinced at the time, he now thinks the consultant's suggestion was the right one. He says I'm much more relaxed about the whole business since I'm sharing Naomi's care, and with any luck I'll conceive again soon.'

As Fran continued the journey home her thoughts were for Jenny, who would so love a child of her own. Nature didn't get it right every time, and yet, although she hadn't planned on having a child herself, she wouldn't want to be without Naomi now.

She spent a contented couple of hours, bathing, playing with and feeding Naomi, before the little girl's drooping eyelids indicated she was ready for bed.

It was nearly nine by the time she settled, and Fran had just wandered down to check the fridge and see what she could find to eat herself when she heard a car pull up outside.

She checked through the door viewer and was surprised to see Cal, walking up the drive.

When she opened the door, he greeted her. 'Hi, I thought I'd check you're OK.'

She felt an idiotic warmth spread through her at his interest.

'I'm fine, thanks.'

She didn't invite him in so he went on to explain, 'I was worried in case this afternoon's faint was a symptom of something more serious, but I can see there's no problem so I won't interrupt your evening.'

'Oh, do come in.' Swamped by conflicting emotions, she removed the door chain. 'Naomi's only just settled and I'm going to make myself a snack. You're welcome to join me.'

'The last thing I want to do is to make more work for you.'

Unused to such consideration, Fran muttered, 'I'm only offering an omelette and salad.'

'Sounds great. Anything I can do?'

'How about the salad?' Fran was already cracking eggs into a basin.

'My speciality,' he told her with a grin. 'I make a mean mixed salad.'

They worked in contented silence and Fran set the small table with a cloth and cutlery. 'Sparkling or still water? I'm afraid I've nothing else.'

'I've a bottle of red wine in the car. I'll get it.'

While he was gone she couldn't help wondering if the wine was there because he'd hoped to be invited in.

She searched out a couple of wine glasses, which hadn't been used since Daniel's day, and rinsed the dust from them, then watched as Cal deftly removed the cork and set the bottle on the table to breathe. 'Before we eat, could you direct me to the bathroom?'

Fran did so, and at the same time pointed out Naomi's room.

When she was ready to serve up the meal he poured the wine. 'Mmm, that's lovely,' Fran murmured, after she had taken her first sip. 'Very fruity.'

She handed him the salad bowl and was soon aware that not eating alone could make the food taste so much nicer.

'I don't think I've ever been served such a light and fluffy omelette.'

'My speciality,' she joked, repeating his earlier words. 'A top chef taught me the secret.'

'A top chef, eh? And where did you meet up with such an important personage?' he teased.

'That would be telling, wouldn't it?'

He laughed. 'And you're not going to?'

'No.'

When they'd finished, she made them both coffee. After a few moments' silence Cal asked hesitantly, 'Did—did your husband—Daniel—did he know you were pregnant?'

She nodded numbly.

'But he still went?'

'His flight was booked when I got the result of my test. The aid agency said they would find a replacement as soon as they possibly could. I encouraged him to go. It would have broken his heart to let the refugees down.

'He suggested delaying the flight until we were married, but it takes so long to arrange unless we'd opted for a special licence and we certainly couldn't afford that.

'I was proud of his dedication. I knew Daniel and I didn't want to stop his last trip because I knew he wouldn't go again. Working for an aid agency is not for men with responsibilities.

'As I saw him off at the airport I had a sudden premonition that I wouldn't see him again. I wanted to beg him not to go but I knew I mustn't.'

Cal rested his huge hand lightly over hers. 'I can't believe... It must have been a dreadful time for you.'

The unexpected contact lit a touch-paper in Fran's nerve endings, causing fireworks to explode throughout her body, and for a moment her confused mind mistook Cal for Daniel. When she could again think straight she was acutely aware of the effect Cal's solicitude was having on her.

Seeing that he was waiting for her to reply, she took a steadying breath. 'I think he must have had some sixth sense about his trip as well. He asked the agency, should anything happen to him, to pay any insurance and money owing to me.'

Cal shook his head in disbelief. 'He was a doctor?'

Fran nodded silently.

'So, do his parents know about his daughter?'

'They're both dead. They were middle-aged when he was born.'

'What did your parents say?'

'They were abroad. I didn't want to worry them and felt sure they would press me to have an abortion or have the baby adopted. I wasn't prepared to do either so I decided this was the best way. I knew I could cope.'

'You went all through your pregnancy and Naomi's birth on your own?'

'I might not have relatives, Cal, but I have friends. Good friends.'

'Like Jenny?'

Fran nodded. 'Hey, I don't know why I'm telling you all this. It must be the wine talking.'

'I'm very honoured that you've told me,' he said quietly.

He appeared completely at ease—which was more than Fran felt, although she had to admit that she was experiencing the same empathy between them as the day they'd first met.

She smiled. 'I supposed I owed it to you when you'd gone to the trouble to check that Naomi and I were OK.'

He took both her hands in his. 'Seeing that smile return to your face is more than enough repayment.'

She looked up and met his gaze watching for her reaction to his words. She nodded her acknowledgement with an aplomb she was far from feeling, especially when she caught a hint of tenderness in his expression as he said, 'I noticed Naomi has a similar smile. She'll be a heart-breaker one day.'

Recognising the oblique compliment from this man about whom she knew so little, Fran tried to hide her lack of composure by saying, 'Coping alone with Naomi growing up is not something I want to think about as yet.'

He acknowledged her response with a sigh, then, loosing her hands, said, 'You have to be at work early in the morning. I must go.' He leaned forward to touch the skin on her forehead with his lips. 'Thank you for trusting me enough to tell me about Naomi's father, and thank you for the omelette—it was delicious. I'll see you Monday, no doubt.'

'I have a day off. I'll be in again on Tuesday.'

'Enjoy your day with Naomi, then.'

'I will, don't you worry.'

As she heard his car driving away Fran pondered his

almost abrupt exit. She'd hoped to learn a little more about him, but her remark about Naomi growing up appeared to have sent him scurrying away.

With a sinking heart she wondered if he had taken it to mean she was looking for someone to share the task. Groaning at the thought of her uncalled-for candour, she resolved to be more careful if the subject arose in the future.

Her morning shift on Sunday was quiet and so passed slowly, allowing thoughts of Cal full rein in her mind. She'd certainly enjoyed the meal they'd made together, but she mustn't read too much into it. He'd come to check she was OK after her faint and his kiss had been nothing more than a thank-you for the meal. Wasn't it?

If only she knew if he was married, or at least had a regular partner, but that seemed to be information he wasn't keen to divulge. To anyone.

Nevertheless, she was looking forward to seeing him again as she arrived for the Tuesday morning early shift and hurried to the office when she saw him arriving.

As she entered he was replacing the telephone receiver. Although he looked up at her entrance, her smile of welcome wasn't returned.

'Is—is everything all right?'

'No. There seems to have been something of a bungle—'

'With one of the patients?' Fran broke in breathlessly.

He shook his head. 'This mistake was made some time ago.'

Frowning, she started to ask, 'What—?'

'If Personnel had been more thorough with their checking, Dr Jenner would never have been employed here as a locum.'

'Why's that?'

'His recent references have just come through, and it appears his standard of work has dropped dramatically from his early days as a doctor. He's not exactly been consci-

entious recently. He could be in for the high jump after this
latest escapade.'

Remembering the note under her windscreen-wiper, Fran
inhaled sharply. She'd hoped to hear nothing more about
the incident and she was determined to prevent any developments that might necessitate her giving evidence.

'Wh-what do you mean ''the high jump''?'

'He'll certainly have to explain his behaviour here, and
I would imagine his professional body will be involved.'

'That seems a bit hard, doesn't it?'

He frowned, obviously surprised by her defence. 'Not if
he makes a habit of it.'

'But—but perhaps he was busy elsewhere in the hospital
when I called him, or there might be any of a hundred
reasons—'

'For him not turning up the next day either? Come off
it, Fran.'

'He should at least be given a chance to defend himself.'
Fran's retort was heated.

'I can assure you, he will,' Cal told her coolly.

Recognising that he was puzzled by her stance, Fran tried
to steady her thoughts and offered him a cup of coffee.

'That would be great, thanks.'

He lounged back in the armchair and studied her intently
as she handed it to him. She met his gaze with an equanimity that belied her growing internal turmoil.

Embarrassed by her outburst, Fran started to sort through
the mail that had collected over the past couple of days.

As he had predicted, amongst the envelopes was an invitation to Mrs Wood's dinner party. She pushed it in his
direction. 'Seems you were right.'

'You asked Jenny?' Cal asked as he recognised the writ-
ing.

'No. I don't count my chickens!'

'But I told you—'

'I didn't expect—'

Cal shook his head. 'Don't you ever believe what you're told?'

'Not without proof. By the way, which other nurses will be there?'

'Does it matter?'

'Only that I don't want to mention it to Kelly or Michelle if they're not invited.'

'The safest thing is not to, then.'

Fran sighed. His deliberate evasiveness was increasing her suspicion that it wasn't as usual as he'd claimed for the nursing staff to be invited. But why should he bother? Was it purely because he thought it good for their working relationship or did he not have a partner to take or was there another, more obscure reason, perhaps personal?

Without having consciously thought about it, she realised that she would like to believe so, and that his reason involved her. She drained her coffee-cup hurriedly and floundered. 'I—I can't sit here all morning. I've work to do even if you don't.'

Cal nodded. 'Unfortunately, I have. But, first, promise you'll ask Jenny today.'

'I said I would, didn't I?' Fran experienced faint exasperation at his insistence.

As she went about her morning's work, she couldn't help feeling just a little flattered. Especially when someone like Cal would surely have at least one ongoing relationship, if not a string of girls in tow.

When she collected Naomi later in the day Jenny readily agreed to babysit on Friday. •

Strengthening her belief that Cal was determined she should attend the get-together, the first thing he did when she arrived on duty on Wednesday afternoon was to ask, 'Babysitter arranged?'

'Yes.'

'I'll pick you up about a quarter to nine.'

Fran countered. 'I can drive myself.'

Cal shrugged. 'But why bother if someone is willing to do the driving instead?'

She had no idea where he lived or whether it would be out of his way to pick her up. 'I—I don't want to put you to any trouble.'

'Actually, Pam Wood's house isn't easy to find in the dark so she asked if I would mind.'

Fran's heart plummeted as she realised it probably hadn't been at his instigation she'd received the invitation after all. 'In that case, I accept.'

'That's all I wanted to know. I must dash to Outpatients now.'

Fran saw only fleeting glimpses of him for the remainder of her shift, but she was relieved that he seemed to have forgotten all about her outburst in support of Dr Jenner.

She saw more of him during her late duty on Thursday. Kelly had wanted to go to the ballet so they had changed shifts. By mid-afternoon Fran decided she had the better part of the bargain. The patients were all comfortably settled and she was able to get on with her routine work, undisturbed.

When Callum came to check that all was well Fran sensed that his trust in her competence was growing, and she hoped fervently that nothing would happen to destroy it.

Her wish wasn't granted. When he'd finished his coffee Cal leaned back and, watching her thoughtfully, said, 'I'm afraid your defence of Dr Jenner was in vain. The agency who represent him want the matter taken further.'

Determined not to react this time, she chewed hard on her bottom lip before she said, 'So, what's going to happen?'

'He's been asked for his side of the story. I don't think he's replied as yet.'

With Dr Jenner now aware that the matter wasn't closed, Fran had a sudden urge to ring Jenny and check that Naomi was OK. The moment Cal left the office to have a chat with a patient she did so.

Her relief was palpable as she heard Jenny say that all was normal. 'Is there a problem? You don't usually ring.'

'I know. I had this silly feeling. Give her a kiss for me and I'll be along about half nine.'

Cal walked back into the office as she was finishing her call, and he watched her replace the receiver with a frown. 'Why do you leave her there if you can't trust your friend?'

Fran was flustered. 'Of course I trust her. It's just me, well, I like to know everything's OK. Wouldn't any mother?' She knew she was burbling incoherently and, without waiting for an answer, returned to completing her report for the night nurses, but Cal wasn't going to let the matter drop so easily.

'Don't you have any family in the area?'

Fran shook her head. 'As I said, my parents are abroad.'

'What does your father do?'

'He works for an oil company and, as you know, they've had their problems recently.'

'Brothers or sisters, then?'

'No,' Fran answered abruptly, wondering why the sudden inquisition.

'Then do you think you might seriously be in danger of becoming over-protective?'

Fran gasped at the accusation. 'You don't understand. It's still very early days—give me a chance.'

He lifted both eyebrows and sighed. 'OK. If you've no problems with the patients, I'll be off.' She sensed his hurt at her rebuff of what had clearly been his idea of an olive branch.

'They're all fine.'

It's just me that has the problem, she wanted to cry to his unyielding back view, but she couldn't and she was desolate. If only she could discover a little more about him, perhaps she would be able to confide in him.

But could she trust him? She knew he was still suspicious of her defence of Dr Jenner, but if she told him about the note on her windscreen he would surely insist that the matter be taken further. And that was the last thing she wanted to happen. For Naomi's sake as well as her own.

Throughout her Friday morning shift Cal's manner was so distant that she half expected him to say the dinner invitation was withdrawn, but, apart from discussing the patients, his only words to her were as she left. 'I'll collect you later as arranged.'

She read the suspicion in his eyes, however, and wished she could tell him the truth, but Naomi was far too important to her for that.

She was late off duty and when she called to collect her daughter Jenny suggested she leave her there, rather than unsettling her for a couple of hours.

'I suppose that's wise. Then I can treat myself to a long and luxurious soak before I get ready.'

She accepted Jenny's invitation to have a cup of tea and spend some time with Naomi while she drank it.

It was barely half past eight when her doorbell rang. Still undecided as to which outfit to wear, Fran slung her dressing-gown over her naked body and ran lightly down the stairs. She did not remove the chain and opened the door the permitted chink.

'Hi. I think I'm early.' Cal looked absolutely stunning in a charcoal grey suit and a white shirt, topped by a bow tie decorated with bold musical symbols.

'Er, sorry. You'd better come in.' As she released the chain Fran felt her colour rising but, despite her state of undress, she couldn't leave him, standing on the doorstep.

She showed him into the living room. 'Drink?'

He shook his head. 'Not at the moment, thanks.' Fran sensed his eyes hadn't missed her nakedness and she drew her dressing-gown closer. Her movement caused him to look round the room. 'No babysitter?'

'Naomi's staying with Jenny overnight.' The moment she'd said it Fran regretted her truthfulness. He might interpret it as an invitation for when they returned from the dinner party. And that was the last thing she had intended.

He made no comment, but she noted a surprised lift of an eyebrow as he picked up the free local newspaper on her coffee-table. 'Take your time. There's no rush.'

Fran sped upstairs and firmly closed her door. There was no longer the luxury of choosing exactly the right outfit. She threw on the one nearest to her. It was a simple midnight blue silk and she piled her hair onto the top of her head to match its sophistication.

As she ran down the stairs he came out of the living room to meet her. Fran could see the surprise in his eyes as he took her hand. 'You look stunning. So different from when you're working.'

Fran acknowledged the compliment with a shy smile. 'I don't think this outfit would be too practical for the geriatric unit.'

He laughed. 'Maybe not practical, but it would do wonders for the male patients! They'd all be back on their feet in no time.'

She raised a wry eyebrow. 'I could say the same for the female side if they saw you dressed like that.' She grinned. 'Does the bow tie indicate musical talent?'

'I certainly like music, and I play the piano, but I'm not a virtuoso. I don't have enough time to practise.' He took the jacket she was carrying and draped it round her shoulders. 'Ready?'

A warmth stole over her at the return of his easy manner towards her. She nodded and drew her jacket close against the icy chill of the evening as Cal closed and secured her front door behind them. 'What kind of music do you prefer?'

'All except the most raucous of sounds that are played on *Top of the Pops*. My taste is eclectic. What about you?'

By this time he was helping her into the passenger seat of a BMW that gleamed under the streetlights.

'Much the same. I don't play, though.'

He nodded and walked round to the driver's side. 'Not even a recorder at school?' he teased.

'Oh, yes. I had a go at one of those and I even had piano lessons for a few months at boarding school. But I soon gave up.'

'Boarding school? Where was that?'

'Dorset.'

'That wasn't your home?'

'No. I was actually born in London. Dad was working at the head office of the oil company at the time. After that he was mostly abroad and wanted Mum with him. She thought I'd be better off with a stable education.'

'You don't sound as though you agreed.'

Fran shook her head. 'I think I'd have preferred being with a loving family.' She changed the subject abruptly. 'Where's *your* home?'

'I was born in Perth.'

'Is it still your home?'

'Afraid not. Home is wherever I happen to be working.'

'You've no family?'

He laughed. 'Not to my knowledge. I think the first thing I need is a wife, but I've been too busy forging a career to think about marrying.'

Although secretly warmed by his response, Fran decided he was avoiding revealing the whole truth. He might not be married, but he could be living with someone. 'So, why did you leave Scotland?'

'There was nothing to keep me there. Dad had died before I went to Glasgow University and Mum died before I qualified.'

'I'm sorry.'

He smiled. 'You needn't be. It was all some time ago.'

How strange, Fran thought. It's almost as if we're both drifting aimlessly without an anchor and fate has decreed that our paths should collide.

'We're nearly there.' Cal's Scottish burr broke in on her reverie.

Fran looked around her. Pam Wood's house certainly wouldn't have been easy to find. The approach was a narrow lane between two detached bungalows, and when Cal drew up in front of a stone-built mansion Fran gasped. 'What a fantastic house.'

He nodded. 'You must see it in the daylight some time. The views from the back are unbelievable. It wasn't in this state when they moved in, though. Pam and her husband have worked hard to renovate the place.'

'How does she find the time? And the energy? I'd have thought being a consultant was hard enough.'

'Her husband has seen to most of it. He's the managing director of a local building firm.'

'That explains a lot!'

Cal rang the bell and the front door was opened by the consultant herself.

'It's very kind of you to invite me, Mrs Wood,' Fran said with a smile.

'Call me Pam, dear. And this is my husband, Lionel. It's lovely to see you both. Dinner's nearly ready. A quick drink first?'

She led the way into a room so big that even the large Victorian pieces and chintz furnishings made no impression on the airy, spacious feeling.

As she poured the gin and tonic they'd both requested, Cal greeted the other members of the geriatric team and their partners, while Fran searched in vain for a sight of any other member of the nursing team.

When they were called almost immediately through to

the dining room, and Fran discovered she was seated next to Cal, her suspicions surfaced again.

He surely *had* planned this! The invitation and the seating arrangements. But why would he bother? As everyone took their seats she realised that most were married couples and decided the most likely reason for her invitation was that Cal hadn't wanted to go to the dinner alone.

She didn't get a chance to puzzle over it any longer, however. Cal was an unbelievably easy person to talk to when he put his mind to it, and over the first course he certainly did, his conversation covering a wide range of topics. So much so that she forgot the presence of the general practitioner who was also a clinical assistant at the hospital. He was seated on her left, and as his wife chattered to Lionel Wood he was closely examining the label on the nearest wine bottle.

As the appetisers were cleared and the leek and Stilton soup was served, she turned to him with a smile of apology. 'I'm sorry. I'm ignoring you.'

He was rotund with slightly greying hair and Fran guessed he was approaching middle age, but that didn't excuse the over-indulgent paternalism of his response. 'Don't you worry, my dear. You two young things must have lots to talk about.'

Fran began to feel uncomfortable. What had the remainder of the guests been told about her? Did they all accept her as Cal's partner? He'd certainly given no indication to her that that was what he'd intended, but neither had the consultant welcomed her as a member of the geriatric team!

Despite her uncertainty, she made up her mind to accept the evening for what it was and enjoy herself.

'Cheese?' A deep voice on her left enquired.

'Oh…er…yes, thanks.' Fran took the proffered dish and helped herself, before passing it on to Cal.

After coffee and after-dinner mints they moved through to the drawing room where the initial drinks had been served. Cal introduced her to those she didn't already know, and conversation flowed freely.

By the time they took their leave Fran was certain the invitation had been Cal's idea. Work hadn't been mentioned once, and although they were all friendly she hadn't seen much evidence of learning to pull together!

When he'd helped her into the car and had eased himself into the driver's seat, Fran couldn't resist murmuring, 'I didn't notice any team-building.'

'It went on all evening.'

'I must have missed it,' she teased.

'You met several team members you didn't know and their partners.'

Fran laughed. 'Work wasn't mentioned, though.'

'It doesn't have to be. When you have to call one of the others to see a patient you should find it easier, having met first in a social capacity.'

'I suppose so.'

'Remember the night I met you? Neither Rob nor I knew who you were, and you accused me of believing the word of a medic rather than that of a nurse we didn't know anything about.'

'And I was right, wasn't I?'

He didn't speak immediately and she turned to study his profile in an attempt to discover why. He must have known she was watching him because he smiled suddenly and said, 'About Rob, maybe, but even he soon changed his tune, didn't he? Very soon, in fact.'

Again Fran sensed faint disapproval of the familiarity between herself and Rob. 'And you didn't think he should?'

He appeared startled by her question. 'No, of course not.' He swung the car into her drive and cut the engine. 'I'd trust you with any of my patients.'

Sensing a reservation in his statement, she muttered, 'Thank you for that vote of thanks at least.' She paused and then, when he didn't respond, said, 'Would you like a cup of coffee?'

'That would be marvellous.'

While she made the coffee and they drank it she felt his earlier easygoing manner had evaporated. It was almost as if her friendship with Rob and her defence of Dr Jenner had undermined his trust in her. He seemed to be looking around for any sign that she wasn't living there alone with Naomi.

The moment he'd drained his cup he took his leave. 'We both have to be at work early again so I won't keep you from your bed. Goodnight, Fran. Thank you for your company.'

She followed him to the front door. As she pulled the door open he appeared about to speak, then checked himself and with another smile of thanks strode down the drive, leaving Fran to another disturbed night.

She tossed and turned restlessly, trying to decide what to make of Cal's changing attitude towards her.

After ringing Jenny to check on Naomi, Fran made her way to the hospital earlier than usual the next morning. Rob, who had been on the go most of the night, was sitting at her desk, yawning.

'How did the evening go?'

'It was great. Super food, and it was good to meet some of the other members of the team. Pity you couldn't go.'

'I guess you had a late night, then?'

'Not very. I was home by eleven.'

'Alone?' he teased.

'Yes.' Fran was indignant. 'Cal drove me back and came in for a quick coffee, but that's all.'

Rob raised his eyebrows suggestively. 'He must be losing his touch.'

Fran gave him a suspicious glance. 'Are you trying to tell me something? Does he have a habit of taking members of the nursing staff to these events?'

Rob laughed. 'There's only been one since I joined the team.'

Throughout Rob's quick update on the patients Fran couldn't help wondering about the last dinner party Pam had given, so much so that on their return to the office she couldn't resist asking Rob, 'Did Cal take a partner to the do you went to?'

'Why do you want to know?'

Fran spun round at the sound of Cal's voice, and colour flared in her cheeks at her indiscretion. 'I couldn't help noticing I was the only member of the nursing staff at the dinner,' she told him hesitantly. 'It made me wonder if the idea had been yours, rather than Mrs Wood's.'

He threw her a look of wry amusement. 'And knowing if I took a partner to the last dinner would answer your question?'

Embarrassed, Fran tried to evade a direct answer. 'If you'd taken another member of the nursing staff as your partner, yes, I think it would.'

He smiled and shook his head. 'We'd better beg to differ, then. Actually, I was unable to go to the dinner Rob attended so he can't be of any help. If you wish to know anything more about me, though, please don't hesitate to ask.'

His sarcasm made Fran wince inwardly. Why had she been so stupid as to question Rob? She should have learnt her lesson after the time Cal had overheard her telling Rob he should be off duty.

Ignoring Fran, he turned to Rob. 'Anything to report this morning?'

'Fran came round with me and made a note of any changes. She'll update you. I'm off now.'

As she repeated Rob's instructions Fran felt a tension between them. She guessed Cal was annoyed at being talked about behind his back, especially when he was still suspicious of her unexpected defence of Dr Jenner.

Hopefully, once he replied to the allegations that would be the end of the matter and she would not hear his name again.

That wasn't to be. During her Monday late shift, when they were both seated at the office desk, Cal leant forward and shattered her peaceful afternoon. 'I suppose you've heard already that Dr Jenner has been reported to the G.M.C. and that you'll probably be asked to tell them what happened with Mrs Dubarry.'

'No...no. I haven't. Why—how did you find out?'

'Mrs Wood told me. As one of the main participants, I thought Personnel would have been in touch with you.'

Fran swallowed heavily. 'No. I've heard nothing since that evening, apart from what you've told me.'

CHAPTER FOUR

FRAN'S head was already spinning wildly when Cal continued. 'Apparently, Jenner could be struck off this time.'

Having tried to convince herself that she'd heard the last of the affair, Fran felt miserably nauseous.

'Wh-why?'

He frowned. 'Why do you think?'

'The post-mortem? Was there a problem?'

'We don't know yet. The pathologist is waiting for some test results.'

'What *did* he find, then?'

'Nothing of any consequence, I gather, but he wants to make absolutely sure before he commits himself.'

Fran shuddered. 'Whatever happens, I—I can't give evidence.'

He stared at her, aghast. 'There's no problem, is there? You made notes about it on the same evening. You said so.'

Fran couldn't answer immediately, but she knew the colour had drained from her face. Yes, she had made careful notes and written down precise timings, but there was no way she could produce them now for fear of what might happen to her daughter.

Neither could she explain her problem to Cal. She was trapped and she could feel his fragile trust in her rapidly evaporating.

'I...er...I meant to, but I never found the time.'

'When I spoke to you that evening you said you'd already made rough jottings and—'

'I had,' she broke in, flinching at his icy tone, 'but they

must have been thrown away. We were so busy,' she added lamely.

Cal clearly wasn't impressed. 'Surely you could have written them up again from memory.'

'So much happened that evening, I can't exactly remember.'

Her answer clearly disappointed him. 'I expected you to co-operate, not to be obstructive.'

'I'm not.'

'You're making a very good attempt at it.'

Cal suddenly seemed to sense her distress, and lowered his voice. 'Look. If it's testifying that's worrying you, I can assure you it's nothing to worry about. All you'll have to do is repeat what you told me on that fateful Tuesday.'

'Please, try to understand. I—I can't remember—'

His disappointment was replaced by an unremitting anger. 'I think you can, but for some reason you don't want to. Don't you think we've enough problems without this? All I can assume is that you didn't call him as you said or, even worse, perhaps you don't want to implicate him.'

'How dare you?' Unable to accept that he could really mean what he was saying, Fran was aghast as well as hurt by his accusation.

She watched his anger carving hard lines on his face and it tore her apart. Just as she was gaining his confidence and respect, she was being forced to forfeit it by someone she didn't know and for some reason she didn't understand.

'I stupidly expected much more of *you*.'

'In what way, might I ask?'

'In every way. I'm pretty sure I can trust your work here, but that's as far as it goes.'

'Just what are you trying to say?' she snapped.

He shrugged. 'Loyalty in their relationships appears to be a commodity in short supply with most females I've met.'

'What *are* you talking about?'

She saw distrust and pain in his eyes as he muttered, 'Don't come the innocent with me. You were perfectly willing to implicate that poor locum to save your own skin until you realised it was likely to backfire on you. What was the problem? Were you worried that your evidence would jeopardise his earning power?'

Speechless, Fran had to clench her fists to prevent herself hitting out at him.

When she remained silent he snapped, 'You can't argue with the truth, can you?'

'I can't argue with such senseless drivel, and I can't imagine what the females you've known before can have done to—'

'That's not important,' he broke in abruptly. 'We're talking about Dr Jenner, whom you claim not to know.'

'And it's the truth.' She defended herself hotly.

'Is it? If you're not prepared to say what you know about Mrs Dubarry's death, I can only assume you are covering up for him for some reason.'

'I—I have never, ever, met him.' She banged the desk with her fist to emphasise her words. 'I wouldn't even know what he looks like.'

Fran was desperate. If she gave the evidence he was looking for she daren't contemplate the consequences for Naomi, and yet if she didn't Cal would never believe her again.

His earlier amiability had already been replaced by a cold indifference, and she wanted to explain and beg him not to believe the worst of her, but she knew it was impossible. For Naomi's sake, she had to keep quiet.

She searched his face but she couldn't read what he was thinking. It was all so unfair. And the stupid part was that even if she told the truth about Dr Jenner's absence it would probably have little bearing on Mrs Dubarry's death.

'You were the trained nurse on duty at the time and only you have the information that will be needed. There's no way you can get out of this.' His steel-blue eyes reinforced his fury.

'What I told you was the truth but, please, please, don't ask me to say anything to the enquiry.'

'I'm disappointed in you, Fran. I'd have backed you to the hilt that first day. Now I'm not so sure.' He strode out of the office, leaving her unable to control the tears that had been threatening.

The situation was made even worse when she went out to collect her car from the car park. Under her windscreen-wiper was another note.

With a sinking heart, she knew that Dr Jenner had received the request for his defence and was taking action. The fact that he'd traced her car at the hospital this time must mean he knew her every movement. It was a horrifying thought that sent cold slivers of ice down her spine.

She unfolded the note with shaking hands and read. 'You have been warned. Do not co-operate with any enquiry about Dr Jenner.'

She was unable to move for some minutes, and even when she arrived at Jenny's house she had still not recovered completely from the shock of finding the note.

Frowning, Jenny asked, 'You look awful. Are you sickening for something?'

Fran hugged Naomi close and nuzzled at the soft, sweet smelling warmth. 'I certainly hope not.' There was no way she was going to worry Jenny, by mentioning the notes. 'It's been a hard day, but we'll be here again early tomorrow. Sorry about your morning lie-in, though. Early shift again, but then I've a day off. I can't wait.'

'It'll do you good,' Jenny told her as she watched Fran make her way back to her car.

'It certainly will,' Fran muttered wearily as she drove off with Naomi. 'Oh, Daniel, why did you have to leave me to cope alone? Because I can't.' She rubbed ineffectually at the tears streaming down her cheek. 'Surely things can't get any worse.'

But when she pulled the car to a stop outside the cottage she saw that they could. A shadowy figure was moving round the back of the building. She froze in her seat, a chill of fear running through her veins. Fran was shivering violently. The only thing she could think of was to take Naomi back to Jenny. She'd be safe there, but what could she tell her friend?

Panicking, she fumbled with her gear lever, wanting to get away—anywhere—as soon as she could. Her terror increased when—as she reversed into the gatepost—she saw a dark figure coming from the direction of the back garden towards the car.

Suddenly her security lamp was triggered, and in the resultant pool of light she saw Callum Smith, looking incongruous in his smart suit, walking towards her.

She switched off the engine and rested her head on the steering-wheel, shaking with relief. She tried desperately to compose herself to greet him, but her terror had been so great she was unable to move immediately.

He opened her car door.

'I was wondering where you'd got to.'

'What—what are you doing here?'

'Just after you left I received Mrs D.'s post-mortem result. As death was due to natural causes, and in the pathologist's view there was nothing Dr Jenner could have done to keep her alive, that should be the end of the affair as far as our unit is concerned. You appeared so worried that I thought you'd like to know as soon as possible.'

He was about to move away down the drive, but as she climbed from the car he noticed her pallor for the first time and the fact that she was still shuddering. He grasped her arm firmly. 'Are you all right? What on earth's the matter?'

'I saw your shadow. I—I thought you were an intruder.

I was just about to drive off, but I got hitched up on the gatepost.'

'Were you going to the police?'

'I guess so,' Fran replied without conviction.

'You're in a dreadful state. Here, give me your keys and I'll unlock the door and check that all's well inside.'

Still trembling, but whether from her earlier fear or Callum's touch she couldn't be sure, Fran lifted Naomi from the car and carried her indoors behind him. He closed the door. 'While you sort your daughter out I'll put the kettle on. You look as if you need something to warm you up.'

Although she was greatly relieved by his news, his anger that afternoon had been too corrosive for her to welcome him. She wished he'd go now, and yet how comforting it was to have someone rattling around in her kitchen.

'Coffee?' he offered, when she joined him downstairs.

She nodded. 'Lovely.'

As she took the cup and saucer from him her still shaking hands clattered them together.

He subjected her to an intense scrutiny from eyes that held a mixture of disbelief and compassion as he asked, 'Why were you so frightened?'

Aware that he was not a man who would be easily fooled, she held his glance for as long as she could. 'Because I thought you were a burglar.'

'Why didn't you run next door for help, then?'

Because her neighbour would have contacted the police, but Fran couldn't say so, without revealing the threats that had been made.

He shook his head. 'Something is clearly troubling you, but unless you're prepared to share it I don't see that I can help you.'

She made a determined effort to hide her fear. 'There's nothing to share. It was just seeing your shadow—'

'I think it's more than that, and I can't help wondering

if it's the same thing that made you change your mind about giving evidence at an enquiry.'

'I didn't change my mind. I...'

'Yes?'

'I lost my rough notes. I was afraid of making a mistake.'

He sighed deeply. 'I know I've only known you for a short time, Fran, but unless I was mistaken about you on our first meeting, and I don't think I was, something has changed you in that time. And it's not for the better.'

She didn't answer, but concentrated on drinking her coffee.

He sighed. 'I'm right, aren't I?'

She shrugged stubbornly. 'I'm just tired.'

He shook his head. 'What are you holding back, Fran?'

Refusing to meet his searching eyes, she mumbled, 'I don't know what you're trying to suggest. It's just not been an easy return to work for me.'

'I wish I could believe you.' He waited, and when she didn't answer he shrugged. 'In that case, if you're sure there's nothing else you need a big strong man for, I'll be off.'

She winced at his sarcasm, but all she could say was, 'Thank you for taking the trouble to come round and for making the coffee.'

'Anytime,' he told her ruefully as he started to open the door. 'Goodnight, Fran. Sweet dreams.'

His hand still on the doorlatch, he paused, as if he expected her to say something more—to explain. When she didn't he shrugged, and before she could catch her breath he muttered, 'I'll check there's no damage to your car on the way out.' Then he was gone, closing the door quietly behind him.

Fran didn't move immediately, but asked herself what she was going to do. In just two weeks back at work, she'd accrued more problems than she would have believed possible.

There had been no need for him to come round. She would have seen him early enough the next morning. So why had he bothered? Was he still snooping to see if she was telling the truth about Dr Jenner? Had he expected to find a sign of him here? Or had he really wanted to prevent her worrying a moment longer?

Confused and agitated, she could no longer be bothered to make herself the meal she had planned so she poured herself a glass of milk and took it to bed with a couple of biscuits. She was so tired. Perhaps returning to shift work hadn't been a good idea, but what else could she do?

Before she'd finished the milk her eyelids started to droop, and the next thing she knew was the early morning radio call.

Discovering the light still on, her panic of the previous evening returned and for a moment she was certain someone else was in the room, but when she saw the untouched biscuits and milk she realised she had been so tired she hadn't switched off the light.

When she had taken the report from the night nurse that morning, she found Rob, waiting to see her.

She forced a smile. 'Problems?'

'Not really, but as that was my last night this week I want to get away. It'll be a while before Callum arrives, but I want to make sure he knows what's happening, and I know I can trust you to tell him. Goodness knows who'll be relieving me today.'

His compliment warmed Fran, especially after his initial suspicion and Cal's continuing distrust. Rob lifted several sets of notes from the trolley and Fran jotted down the changes he indicated.

'It's probably better if I introduce you to the new admission personally,' he told her. 'Mrs Chambers was found on the floor beside her bed, suffering from hypothermia.'

'A stroke?'

'I'm not sure. I can't find any sign of weakness or any

other reason for her being on the floor. We've been gradually warming her and she doesn't seem to have any idea
either.'

They walked to the new admission's bed. 'This is the
nurse in charge on this shift, Mrs Chambers. She'll look
after you now.' After checking the patient's observation
chart, he nodded. 'You're doing well.' He turned to Fran.
'I'll leave you to it, then.'

When Callum arrived he found Fran promising to organise someone to look after Mrs Chambers's cat.

'That's not your job,' he murmured tautly as they walked
towards the office.

She shrugged. 'Why not? Knowing the cat's being cared
for will stop worry making her condition worse.'

He gave her a puzzled look but didn't comment further,
and Fran knew it was going to take a long time to recapture
even a modicum of the empathy there had been between
them in the beginning.

She thought about his visit the previous evening. It
hadn't been necessary but if, as he'd said, it had been to
prevent her worrying, and she'd practically thrown him out
of the cottage, what must he think of her?

Over the past couple of days she must have appeared
callous and uncaring to him. No wonder her compassion
for Mrs Chambers's cat was now causing him confusion.
He must think her behaviour unbelievably inconsistent.

Thank goodness she could now put the problem of Dr
Jenner behind her, and hopefully start to prove herself to
Cal once again. Because one thing she was sure of—he was
someone whose respect she would hate to lose permanently.

'I'll just tell you about a couple of changes to treatment
regimes that Rob asked me to let you know about.'

'He's gone for his days off already, I gather.'

Fran nodded and rushed to point out to Cal that they'd
done a quick round of the patients before he'd left.

He subjected her to a long and searching look. 'I'm sure

Rob'd be pleased to know how quickly you leapt to his defence, even though I intended no criticism.' He paused. 'So, if you'd like to update me on what's going on, I'll leave you to get on with your chores and I'll see you to-morrow.'

Cringing at his icy response, she murmured, 'I'm afraid not. I have the day off. And I can't wait.'

'Good for you. Bad for the rest of us.'

'What do you mean?'

'Exactly what I say.' His eyes met and held hers for longer than was necessary. 'It's great to have a reliable member of staff.'

Relieved to discover that he still considered she had *some* good points, Fran accepted his compliment with a nod. But she couldn't banish an insistent question from her mind about his previous relationships. Judging by what he'd said when he'd been so angry with her, he must have been deeply hurt by someone in the past, making him reluctant to trust any female with whom he came into contact.

Fran spent a restful day with Naomi, confident now that the threat to her daughter's safety no longer existed. She wondered vaguely where Dr Jenner had disappeared to, and how the case against him was proceeding, but she didn't really care as long as she didn't have to work with him again or testify against him.

She felt rested when she reported for the early shift on Thursday. After she had taken the report she did a quick round of the patients and was warmly welcomed.

Mrs Chambers called her to the head of the bed and took hold of her hand. 'I want to thank you for seeing about Tommy,' she told Fran weakly. 'The volunteer, who has given him a temporary home, came to see me yesterday. She tells me he's settled well. I'd still be worried about him if it wasn't for you.'

'I just happened to be on the spot at the right time.'

'Dr Smith said it wasn't really your job.'

Fran smiled at her. 'Take no notice. I expect he'd rather I spent my time making him coffee, and that's not my job either. It was no trouble and I was delighted to be able to help.'

'At least I can die happy now.'

'What do you mean?' Fran pulled up a chair and sat close to her patient. 'You're not going to leave that poor cat an orphan. We'll soon have you moving about again and off home.'

Mrs Chambers shook her head. 'You're as bad as Dr Smith. He won't listen either, but I know.' She smiled at Fran. 'It doesn't worry me, you know. I'll see my Harry again. It's been a long time.' She leant back against her pillows and closed her eyes, a smile of contentment smoothing the lines from her face.

After a few moments Fran gently released her hand and quickly completed her ward round.

Cal was in the office, drinking coffee, and as he poured her a cup Fran smiled, remembering what she had said to Mrs Chambers.

'What's the joke?'

Fran thought she detected a defensive tone in his voice and rushed to explain. If he was prepared to return the situation between them to normal, she wasn't about to upset the apple cart again. 'I just told a patient that pouring coffee wasn't my job, but it's not yours either and yet every time I come into the office you ply me with a cupful.'

His smile was unexpectedly compassionate. 'I saw you, talking with Mrs Chambers. I thought you might need it.'

Fran nodded ruefully. 'Do you honestly think we'll get her back on her feet this time?'

He shook his head. 'Not if she doesn't want to, and now her cat is settled she doesn't.'

Fran glared at him indignantly. 'Are you suggesting it's my fault, by any chance?'

He laughed. 'Would I dare?' Then sobering, he added, 'No. She's just suffered one setback too many.'

'It *was* a stroke?'

'Probably a minor one.'

'You mean it was probably a transient ischaemic attack?'

'According to her GP, she's had several TIAs but has refused to be referred for assessment. Possibly because any residual weakness disappeared within a day, and more likely because she just wants to be left alone.'

'She's almost serene now she's made up her mind.'

'She has the strongest faith I think I have ever come across. She doesn't just hope for an afterlife, she *knows* exactly what it'll be like.'

'Mmm. I've met someone like her before.' Fran was thinking of Daniel so her reply was sharper than she'd intended.

Seeing the sudden change in her manner, Cal frowned, but to Fran's relief didn't probe, merely commenting, 'You said yourself how contented she is.'

As they talked about work Fran sensed the atmosphere between them gradually easing. He was certainly less friendly than he had been, but as they started a round of the patients he placed a hand on her arm that sent a remembered warmth surging to her nerve endings.

'How's Mrs Jenkins?' he asked quietly as they approached her empty bed.

'She's had a good night. She's watching television in the day room and seems much happier.'

He nodded. 'We can't keep her here indefinitely, but the same thing will happen if she returns to her empty house. She'll be back again.'

Fran shrugged defensively. 'We're doing what we can. The social workers have been to see her and she's only too willing to move, but there's nothing available that would be suitable.'

'Are they still looking?'

'As far as I know.'

'Does she own her house?'

Fran shook her head. 'That's why sheltered accommodation would be the answer. If she moves to a residential home, someone will have to foot the bill.'

When they entered the day room Mrs Jenkins looked up at their approach. 'Are you going to send me home?'

'Not immediately.' Cal smiled.

Fran watched relief flood her eyes.

Having checked Mrs Jenkins's pulse and listened to her chest, he nodded reassuringly. 'You're definitely on the mend. I'm off this weekend, but we'll see how you are Monday and perhaps make a decision then.'

When they eventually made their way back to the office, Fran was relieved that their discussions about the patients appeared to have purged some of her glaring inconsistencies from his mind.

Another early shift on Friday morning started badly. When Cal arrived she had sombre news for him.

'How about me doing a round of the patients now?'

'Fine. I'll fill you in on most of the changes as we go round. But first I must mention Mrs Chambers. She had another what they thought was a TIA when she went out to the toilet last night, but now we think it's more than that so they moved her up to the first bed.'

'How is she this morning?'

'Not good. She's not responding and Rob couldn't decide if it was purely because she didn't want to. Like you said, she's given up.'

She wheeled the trolley of notes out of the office and followed him to the first bed where Mrs Chambers lay with her eyes closed.

He took the seat beside her and took her hand between his. 'Hello, Mrs Chambers.' When she didn't answer he added, 'Do you remember me? Dr Smith?'

When there was still no reaction he studied her charts

and then indicated he would take a look at her. Fran drew
the curtains around her patient and assisted with a thorough
examination, but he elicited no response. Finally, with a
ruefully raised eyebrow, he jotted down his findings and
they moved on.

'Are you working over the weekend?'

Fran nodded. 'I'm on earlies both days.'

'I'm off but you shouldn't be too busy. Despite pressure
from above, I can only free- up the couple of empty beds
vacated by Mrs Laing and Mrs Ashton today.'

'What about Mrs Laker? Her drug regime seems to have
her heart failure stabilised.'

'I'd rather she stayed in a few more days. Discharging
patients too early inevitably leads to readmission. I'd rather
keep them longer and get it right first time. And, thankfully,
Pam agrees with me.'

Fran nodded approvingly and refilled Cal's coffee-cup.
'What do you want us to do about Mrs Chambers?'

He sighed. 'She seems comfortable so all we can do is
keep her that way. We'll start intravenous feeding but no
other intervention for the moment.'

'Fine. Do you know which house officers are on duty?'

'I believe Gerald will be in tomorrow. I'm not sure about
today. But if there are any problems in that direction, contact Pam Wood immediately. She's on call this weekend.'

'I'll try not to disturb her.'

'She won't mind. Better than trying to deal with emergencies on your own, isn't it?'

Despite their accord when they'd been discussing the patients, Fran now sensed that his words were a warning.

She felt moved to defend herself. 'I suppose you're suggesting I should have contacted either you or Pam Wood
when Dr Jenner didn't appear.'

When he didn't speak, but waited for her to continue,
she muttered indignantly, 'Believe me, I didn't even know
you existed then and had never met Pam Wood. I was told

to contact Dr Jenner in the event of any problems, and that's what I did. It's the house officer's place to decide whether it's necessary to get in touch with a senior member of the team, isn't it?'

He watched her thoughtfully for several slight seconds, then sighed. 'That apparent absence of communication is the reason for Pam's attempts at team-building.'

Fran was scathing. 'It'll take more than a token nurse at her get-togethers to improve things.'

'What do you mean—"token nurse"?'

'Well, I didn't see any of my colleagues, did you?'

'Not this time. It depends on the duty rotas.'

Fran felt she was paddling through treacle, trying to discover the real reason she had been invited. He had no intention of enlightening her, and the sooner she accepted the fact the better. Everything about Callum Smith was a mystery and he seemed determined to keep it that way.

'If there's nothing more you need me for, I have plenty to do.'

'If you don't mind, I'll just finish my coffee then I'll go in search of Pam.' She had tried to hide her exasperation, but his amused response told her she had failed.

When he returned a little later, with the consultant in tow, he came to look for her.

'Pam wants a word with you,' he told her. 'I'll hold the fort here.'

'Come and sit down a moment,' the consultant said. 'Cal says you've had the most to do with Mrs Chambers since her admission. She's given no next of kin, just the name of a neighbour. Has she said anything to you about family?'

'Only that she has no one at all to care about her or her cat. That's why I sorted out a temporary home for him.'

'She hasn't had any visitors?'

'To my knowledge, only the lady who's taken the cat in.'

'Sad isn't it, when people reach the age of ninety without a soul left in the world to care?'

Fran nodded. 'She said the other day she wouldn't get better because she just wanted to be with her husband. He apparently died many years ago.'

'There are so many like her, I'm afraid.' She smiled at Fran. 'I'll get back to my men now but, before I do, Cal tells me you're on duty all weekend. So am I. Don't hesitate to ask for help, will you?'

Fran watched her go with a heavy heart. Was that why she had come to the ward? Had Cal told Pam he was worried about leaving his patients? Had he asked her to reinforce the message that Pam didn't mind being disturbed because he didn't trust Fran?

She could only conclude so. She made her way slowly back to Mrs Chambers's bedside. Cal was seated on one side, chatting quietly to his comatose patient. Shaking his head, he indicated that Fran should pull up the chair beside him. She smoothed the hair back from their patient's forehead then took her hand between her own.

They were both with her when she died. They did what was necessary and then made their way to the office. Fran couldn't prevent a tear trickling down her cheek. Cal saw it and wiped it away with a gently caressing thumb. 'It's what she wanted. Don't be sad.'

Fran breathed deeply. 'I know, but I can't help remembering what she was like when I first saw her.'

'You really care, don't you?'

'Of course I care,' she retorted. 'Why do you think I do the job?'

He smiled. 'For your sanity and those little luxuries like food?'

Her heart lurched uncomfortably at him repeating her words in this context.

He must have sensed her dismay because almost immediately he murmured, 'That was a joke, Fran. You've done more than could be expected of you. She knew her cat was being cared for and that was probably the most important thing any of us did for her.'

She acknowledged his generosity with a shy smile but when, shortly before her shift ended, he left for his weekend off without another word she knew she'd be a fool to believe that episode indicated that anything was altered between them. He'd merely consoled her as he would have anyone who was upset.

She couldn't sleep that night. She thought about the love Mrs Chambers had shared with her husband and wondered why she herself always seemed to get it wrong. Was she destined never to find the right man to share a similar love?

Having worked herself almost to a standstill, lunchtime on Saturday came long before she was ready for it so she missed her own lunch break in order to get the records up to date ready to hand over to the afternoon shift. Even so, she was late off duty because Mrs Chambers's neighbour rang to discuss when she should collect her friend's belongings, and as she clearly wanted to chat, Fran gave her all the time she needed.

She apologised profusely to Jenny for being late when she arrived to collect Naomi.

'No problem,' Jenny told her. 'She's enjoying a trip to the park.'

'Brian's taken her out?'

Jenny laughed. 'And miss his football? You know better than that.'

Fran felt an irrational fear clutch at her heart. 'Who's taken her, then?' she screeched, grasping Jenny's arm.

Her friend backed away. 'Steady on, Fran. She's with Cal. The shops were heaving. When he saw me struggling he said he'd take her round that way to help me.'

Fran clapped her hand to her forehead. 'Oh, I'm sorry, Jenny. I—I don't know what's the matter—'

She was saved from explaining further by Cal, ringing

the doorbell. 'We've fed the ducks,' he greeted them. 'Now it's feeding time for us.'

He looked from one to the other, and Fran knew he sensed the tension between the two friends. 'Sorry if I'm a little late. We were enjoying ourselves too much.'

'I was late as well.' Fran felt so guilty about her outburst that she said, 'I haven't eaten yet either. Can I get you both something?'

Jenny shook her head. 'I grabbed a sandwich when I got in and that's all I want. Brian and I are going for a slap-up meal this evening, paid for by his boss, so I don't want to spoil my appetite.'

That left Cal. Fran knew she couldn't withdraw her invitation, but after all that had happened she expected him to refuse it.

To her surprise, he accepted. '*I'd* like to take you up on your offer.'

'Great. I'll see you at the cottage, then.'

She took Naomi from Jenny's arms and, whispering another apology, carried her daughter out to the car. The moment they were alone Fran vented her anxiety on Naomi. 'Now why do you think he wants to come to lunch with someone he doesn't believe he can trust?'

When Naomi gurgled Fran giggled. 'No, I don't know either, but I get the feeling he is still checking up on me. Good luck to him, then. That's what I say. He won't find Dr Jenner hiding under my bed.'

Cal arrived at the cottage close behind them, and offered to make sandwiches while she played with Naomi. 'I don't want to waste your quality time with her.'

What was he suggesting now? That Naomi was missing out. He never seemed to say anything that didn't contain a hidden meaning.

Once Naomi was settled for a late afternoon nap Fran made them both coffee. Over her cup she watched him surreptitiously as he scanned the few compact discs she possessed.

'You obviously enjoy musicals.'

She nodded.

'Have you seen the one at the Empire at the moment?'

She shook her head. 'It's a long time since I got to a live show.'

'I hear it's very good.'

She smiled. 'Perhaps I could get the CD. They're sure to have produced one.'

'Better than that, how about coming to see the show one day next week? I'm sure Jenny would babysit. She said you don't get out enough.'

Fran glared. 'Have you been discussing me with Jenny again?'

'Not really. She volunteered the information.'

'I don't want to be taken out just because Jenny prescribes it.'

'Don't be so tetchy,' he told her with a teasing smile, 'just because you had a disturbed night again last night.'

'How—? I didn't. I—'

'I expect losing Mrs Chambers upset you.'

Fran sighed. It was true, of course, but that didn't give him the right to confuse her in this way. She wanted him to trust her, not to feel sorry for her. And much as she enjoyed his company, she still knew very little about him. Except that he'd taken a shine to Naomi and, that being so, seemed to think it was his mission in life to look after her mother.

In that he was like Daniel. A caring person, but without the openness. She never quite knew what he was thinking about anything.

'So, do you think Jenny would babysit?'

'I could ask her, I suppose.' After all, it was only a theatre outing, which she knew she would enjoy. 'I'm off Tuesday and Wednesday next week.'

'I'll see if there are any tickets available. Any preference as to which night?'

Fran drained her coffee-cup. 'Tuesday would be better as I'm on the early shift Thursday morning.' She yawned. 'Which reminds me—I am tomorrow as well. And I still have a lot of chores to catch up on.'

'I can take a hint. I'm just on my way.' He smiled, and as they walked to the door he murmured his thanks. 'Till Tuesday, then.'

He searched her face and leant towards her to drop a light kiss on her forehead. 'Take care.' He touched her arm, and opening the door, was gone before she could recover from a yearning for him that she was finding difficult to control.

She watched his car out of sight, wondering if he had any idea how confused she felt. Or was he just as confused? Despite their acrimonious week, she felt a definite attraction towards him when he turned on the charm as he had just done. And she couldn't help wondering if it was a good thing. At least his invitation to the theatre told her that he didn't have a commitment to someone else. Or did it? She shook her head, trying to clear it of the contradictory messages with which Callum had been filling it since the day they'd met.

CHAPTER FIVE

THERE had been no admissions overnight, and when Fran did her ward round on Sunday morning she was pleased to find the condition of her remaining patients stable and improving. It was about time she had a peaceful shift.

Fran was just enjoying a cup of coffee when Pam Wood put in an appearance. 'All well?'

Fran rested her hand superstitiously on the wooden desk. 'So far. No admissions and no problems.'

Pam settled herself in one of the armchairs. 'Any of that coffee going?'

'Plenty.' Fran poured a fresh cup and handed it to the consultant, then searched for something to say. 'That was a lovely meal you gave us last week.'

'You enjoyed yourself?'

'Very much.'

'Did Callum?'

'I...er...I think so.'

'I hope so. He works himself too hard. I had to be quite firm to make him take another weekend off. He thinks we can't manage without him. I do hope he's gone right away.'

Fran sighed. 'I don't think so. He took my daughter to the park yesterday.'

She sensed Mrs Wood was about to ask something more, then changed her mind and concentrated on finishing her coffee. Fran was grateful. She was so confused herself by Cal's changing manner towards her that she wouldn't have known the answer anyway.

'That was very welcome, thanks, Fran. I'll be around if you need anything. Anything at all. Don't hesitate to contact me.'

Fran was thoughtful when she was left alone, sure now that Cal had asked the consultant to keep a close eye on her. She couldn't help wondering if the reason he had been unwilling to take time off had been because he thought she couldn't be trusted, especially when working with locums.

Towards the end of Fran's shift Mrs Chambers's neighbour arrived to collect her friend's belongings. The neighbour was nearly as frail as Mrs Chambers had been.

'She asked me to arrange for her bungalow to be cleared if anything happened to her,' she confided.

'That won't be easy. Will you be able to manage, or would you like some help?'

'The warden's going to help me.'

'Mrs Chambers was in sheltered housing?'

She nodded. 'It's a development of small bungalows. Very comfortable.'

'Council-owned?'

'No. We rent them from a church organisation. They're very good to us.'

Thinking of Mrs Jenkins's need, Fran asked, 'Is there a waiting list?'

She shrugged. 'I suppose so, but I wouldn't know. The warden could probably tell you.'

'I'm off duty shortly. Perhaps I could run you back home with these things and speak to her. We have a patient here who needs a home where there's someone who can keep an eye on her.'

'I *would* appreciate a lift back.'

'Take a seat in our day room and have a cup of tea with the patients. The trolley's doing the rounds at the moment.'

Having handed over to the oncoming shift, Fran quickly rang Jenny. 'I'm going to be a little late. Is that a problem?'

'Not at all. Take your time. I hope it's that gorgeous Cal, delaying you.'

'No... He's not working today.'

'Pity.' Jenny's rejoinder was amused. 'I'm sure he has a thing about you.'

'Rubbish,' Fran demurred, aware that yesterday he had seemed prepared to forgive and forget.

She went in search of her passenger. When they arrived at the small development she was surprised how pleasant Mrs Chambers's little bungalow was. The warden promised to bear Mrs Jenkins in mind when the board of trustees met to discuss the vacancy.

'Is there a secretary or someone we could contact as well?'

The warden gave her a name and telephone number.

Fran made her way to collect Naomi with optimistic excitement. As it was Sunday there was nothing she could do so she enjoyed her time with Naomi. Not being on duty until the late shift on Monday, she even managed a brief lie-in the next day.

Having fed Naomi, she made herself a substantial brunch then carefully checked her appearance in the mirror before she left for work. She was wearing the same navy A-line skirt that she always wore on duty, but she had searched out one of her better blouses, an emerald green cotton, which, she knew, contrasted well with her dark colouring. She would feel more confident in Cal's presence, knowing she looked her best.

She asked Jenny if she'd be able to look after Naomi the next evening, but stressed that it might not be necessary if there were no tickets available.

Jenny agreed, her eyes shining. 'Surely Callum will take you somewhere else if they're not.'

Fran protested. 'Who said it was Cal I was going with?'

'No one. I just guessed.' Jenny grinned, hugging Naomi to her. 'I'm right, aren't I?'

Fran had to admit she was, and before her friend could enthuse any longer she checked her watch, saying, 'I must dash.'

The first thing she did, after taking the report and doing a quick round of her patients, was to telephone the social worker dealing with Mrs Jenkins's case and give her the information she had gleaned from the warden of the sheltered housing. She was replacing the receiver when Cal came into the office.

Believing she could read a guarded expression in his eyes, Fran was formal in her greeting. 'Good afternoon, Cal.'

'Hi. All quiet?'

'So far so good.'

'Surprisingly, we still have three empty beds. In fact, it's about to go up to four as I've decided Mrs Laker can go home.'

'She's done well, hasn't she?'

He nodded. 'I just have to convince her GP of the fact in my discharge letter. She really didn't need to be admitted last week.'

'She came in during the night so she was probably seen by a locum who didn't know her and maybe had no access to her notes.'

'No doubt you're right.' His eyes lit up with a sudden gleam. 'If it was necessary, I hope you'd defend me as readily as you defend everyone else.'

Fran felt her cheeks flood with colour. 'I try to see both sides of any argument.'

'And give those who don't know you the wrong idea?'

Unsure if this was an admission that he now believed the suspicions he had harboured about her had been wrong, Fran shot him a surprised look, before stuttering, 'I—I don't think so...'

'You don't? Hmm. I'm not sure if I agree. But let's not argue about it. Tell me, is Jenny able to look after Naomi tomorrow?'

He hadn't changed his mind, then. 'I think so.'

'You only think. Didn't you ask her?'

Fran nodded, but offered him a way of escape. 'I mentioned it, but said I would confirm if there were still tickets available.'

'There *are* tickets so I'll collect you around seven.'

'I'll look forward to it.'

'We'll eat afterwards if that's OK by Jenny.'

'I'll ask her tonight.'

A frantic buzzing sent them both racing into the ward. Mrs Laker, her eyes wide with horror, had her finger jammed on the nurse call button as she watched Mrs Jenkins struggle hopelessly for breath.

'Just relax, Mrs Jenkins.' Cal's voice was soothing as he turned on the oxygen supply and placed the mask over his patient's face.

Meanwhile, Fran released Mrs Laker's finger and led her gently to the other side of the room.

'I—I just—'

'I'll be back in a moment. You can tell me then.'

She drew the curtains around Mrs Jenkins's bed space and queried, 'Nebuliser?'

Cal nodded. As Fran set off to the treatment room he called, 'With salbutamol.'

She was soon back with an emergency selection of drugs and the machine. Mrs Jenkins's condition was already improving so Cal indicated they wouldn't use it for the moment.

Fran placed the machine within easy reach. 'I'll just check Mrs Laker.'

She crossed the ward and smiled. 'All's well now. Don't worry.'

'I—just—I only, I just told her I was going home. That was all. I didn't do anything else.'

Fran pulled up a chair. 'Of course you didn't. No one can predict when these attacks might occur. I expect she's sorry to see you go. You've got on well together haven't you?'

Mrs Laker nodded, but I saw she was biting her lip nervously.

'Before you leave, you'll be able to see for yourself that she's fine.'

As she spoke, Cal pulled back the curtains around the bed and smiled in their direction, before making his way to the ward office. Fran remained in the ward, keeping a close eye on the asthmatic while carrying out routine tasks.

She was pleased when Mr Laker came to collect his wife, but before she let her go Fran took her across to speak to Mrs Jenkins. She removed the oxygen mask for a moment so that the two ladies could say their goodbyes.

'She looks much better,' Mrs Laker told her as they walked down the ward corridor. 'I was so worried about her.'

'She's in good hands here. And you look after yourself. Don't forget to take those tablets regularly.'

'I certainly won't.'

Fran checked on Mrs Jenkins again and then joined Cal in the office. 'It sounds as if it was the thought she might be discharged, like Mrs Laker, that sent her into the panic.'

Cal sighed. 'I guessed as much. But what can we do? We can't keep her here indefinitely.'

Fran told him about the sheltered bungalow that had been Mrs Chambers's home. 'I told the social worker about it as soon as I came on duty, and the warden has promised to bear Mrs J. in mind.'

Cal looked up at her with admiration. 'Thanks for thinking of her. You're one in a million, Fran. I'd have thought you had enough to do, without chasing around there in your spare time.'

Feeling a warm glow at his appreciation, she said warningly, 'Don't get too excited. There's probably a long waiting list and, anyway, it won't happen overnight. It'll take quite some time for Mrs Chambers's friend to clear the bungalow.'

He nodded. 'I'll keep all my fingers and toes crossed.'

She laughed. 'I hope you'll be able to work that way for what'll probably be quite a time!'

He scrutinised her closely. 'I think you've had more knocks in your short life than is good for you. What you need now is a hefty infusion of optimism. It's not healthy for you to expect things to continue to go wrong. I'll have to see what I can do about it. Perhaps our theatre trip tomorrow will be a good time to start.'

Fran attempted to feign indifference, but the hidden meaning she sensed behind the lightly spoken words made it difficult—especially when his blue eyes crinkled into a smile which caused her pulse to quicken. To give herself a chance to regain her composure, she murmured, 'I must check on Mrs Jenkins again.'

She left him seated in the office, watching her with a lazy smile, and as she walked into the ward her heart skipped a couple of beats. He really had dismissed his earlier distrust of her, a thought which gave her a boost of the optimism he thought she lacked.

'How are you feeling now, Mrs Jenkins?'

Her patient gave her a feeble smile.

'You look much better. Shall we try you without this?'

She nodded so Fran removed the oxygen mask and turned off the supply. 'That's better. I expect your mouth is quite dry now. Would you like a cup of tea?'

'Just a sip of water, thanks.' Her wheeze was still pronounced when she spoke so Fran remained nearby to make sure all was well.

The patients were finishing their evening meal when Cal came in search of her. 'I'm off now. Let me know if there's any problem about tomorrow evening.' He nodded towards Mrs Jenkins. 'You look much better.'

Lifting her chart from the foot of her bed, he checked the prescription sheet. 'We'll continue with the same cocktail of pills and see how you go.' He turned to Fran. 'Dr

Ward is on call tonight. I've had a chat with him so there should be no problem if Mrs Jenkins needs anything.' He smiled in the patient's direction. 'I'll be in first thing in the morning to see you. Sleep well.'

'Good night, Doctor, and thank you.'

As he turned to go Fran detected a quick flicker of an eyelid as he murmured, 'Until tomorrow.'

She didn't return his wink, but she couldn't hide the sensuous smile that touched her lips. Well pleased by her response, he strode jauntily from the ward.

The feeling of excitement he'd left with her carried her through the remainder of her evening shift, and she was still smiling to herself when she rang Jenny's bell.

'My, you look pleased with life,' Jenny greeted her.

'I've the next two days off, haven't I?'

'Is that all? What about your outing tomorrow evening?'

'Cal wants to collect me at seven. Would that be all right by you?'

Jenny nodded. 'Fine. Are you going to bring Naomi here, or would you prefer she stayed in her own bed?'

'Whatever's best for you. He wants us to eat after the show.'

'That's OK. Brian's out and you're not working on Wednesday so it'll be easier if I come over there. I'll get him to collect me.'

'Just before seven, then. If that's OK by you?'

Fran spent a leisurely Tuesday with her daughter. After a morning catching up with the housework, she walked to the shops with Naomi in the buggy. Although the wind was still wintry, the afternoon sun promised the imminent arrival of spring, and as she sauntered through the park her heart sang in tune with the birds who were looking for mates.

The change in Cal's attitude towards her, especially since

the weekend, together with his invitation to the theatre, surely marked a turning point for her.

Naomi utter a sudden yelp of delight as a duck waddled up to them, hoping for food. Fran crouched beside her and pointed out the other ducks, moving hopefully towards them.

Naomi burbled happily for the remainder of the outing and Fran returned to the cottage in time to bath and feed her with a feeling of well-being she hadn't enjoyed since the day she'd returned to work.

It was nearly seven when Jenny arrived, and Fran still wasn't ready so, after hurriedly showing her friend where everything was, she rushed upstairs to change into a suitable outfit for the theatre.

Rejecting leggings as not smart enough, she settled on a long black skirt teamed with a black woollen top decorated with sequins and pearls.

She expected Cal to be early, as he'd been the night of the firm dinner, but it was nearly seven-fifteen before the doorbell rang.

'I'm so sorry, Fran,' he greeted her. 'I was held up at the hospital. To make sure we get to the theatre for the start, I've a cab waiting. I don't want to waste time, searching for a parking space.'

'I'll just let Jenny know we're off.'

He closed the door behind her when she'd said goodbye and helped her into the waiting taxi. 'You look great,' he told her as his eyes slid appreciatively over her outfit. 'I think we're going to enjoy this evening.'

The show was a revival of *Oklahoma!* by a regional company, but over a glass of wine at the interval they both agreed it couldn't have been done better.

'That dark-haired chap has a fantastic voice, doesn't he?' Fran enthused. 'And he's so good-looking. He'll surely be a star one day.'

'Handsomer than me—or the morning television presenter?' he teased.

'I wouldn't go as far as to say that.'

He laughed. 'I'm pleased to hear it. I was becoming madly jealous.'

She joined in his laughter. 'I don't see why when all the female patients swoon over you.'

'I think I'd prefer it if they were just a little younger.' He grinned. 'That's why I quite appreciated finding you at my feet at the antique fair.'

Fran's cheeks coloured rapidly. 'I had no idea you were there.'

He laughed. 'You didn't? Another fantasy blown! And I was so enjoying reliving it.'

The theatre bell rang as she joshed, 'I don't believe a word of it. You just enjoyed the opportunity to tell everyone around you were a doctor!'

He squeezed her waist threateningly as he led her back to her seat. 'How could you be so doubting? That's the last time I come to your rescue.'

The memory of their light-hearted banter bathed Fran in warm contentment as the curtain lifted for the second act.

When the show finished he asked her, 'Where shall we eat?'

'I—I'm not sure what's around these days. You choose.'

He took her arm as they negotiated the theatre steps. 'I suppose you haven't been out for a meal since Naomi was born?'

'No.' She didn't add, nor for some long time before that, but it would have been true.

'Italian all right? There's a very good one opened nearby.'

'Lovely.'

As the crowds thinned he slung his arm around her waist and pulled her close. 'What a beautiful night, even if it is chilly.'

'It's been a fantastic day. I took Naomi to the park. She was fascinated by the scavenging ducks. Pity I didn't think to take some bread crusts with us.'

'There's a whole summer ahead for that.'

'I know, and I'm looking forward to it. I had a lovely day with her today.'

'It's a pity you can't spend more time with her.'

Fran shrugged. 'Perhaps I appreciate the time I do have with her more.' She met his penetrating gaze with a smile that was meant to be reassuring but which she could see didn't convince him.

Wanting to prevent him commiserating, she said brightly, 'There are some delicious smells making me suddenly very hungry. Are we nearly there?'

His tightening arm around her waist told her that he understood. 'This is it.'

He pushed open the door of The Pasta House and led her into a warm and steamy environment.

'Mmm—fresh bread. Lovely.'

They were shown to a corner table and Cal asked her what she would like to drink.

'Another glass of red wine, I think.'

'I'll join you. I'll get a half-carafe.'

'One glass will be plenty for me,' warned Fran with a smile.

'That's OK. I'm not driving,' he told her as the waiter arrived with a half-carafe of Chianti. 'Now, what to eat with the wine?'

'The seafood cannelloni sounds good. I think I'll settle for that.'

Cal smiled at the waiter. 'Make that two.'

'Very good, sir.'

Cal filled their glasses with the wine and lifted his to his lips. 'Cheers. Here's to the next show.'

'I'll drink to that,' she murmured as their glasses clinked.

The waiter arrived with some of the freshly baked crusty batons that smelled so delicious. 'Your food won't be long.'

They both sampled the bread and Fran said, 'I've missed this. I used to bake my own when I wasn't working.'

The moment she'd said it she realised the danger.

'You don't have the time now?'

'I'd rather devote it to Naomi.' Deliberately avoiding his gaze, she concentrated on her glass of wine as she spoke.

'I'm not surprised. Perhaps you ought to get one of the automatic bread-makers that are on the market.'

Fran wrinkled her nose. 'I don't believe the results would be as good as this. Anyway, kneading the dough is the best part. I always feel better after a bread-making session.'

'Like the Japanese who vent their frustration on dummies?'

Fran laughed. 'That's exactly it.'

She was aware of him, watching her closely, 'You're a home-maker rather than a career girl, aren't you?'

This time she met his gaze and her eyes were caught and held. Unsure if he was complimenting or criticising her, she felt her chest muscles tighten with panic—and another emotion to which she didn't want to admit. 'I—I don't think so. I—'

She was relieved to be prevented from completing her sentence by the arrival of the food.

'This is good,' she told him.

'What's the herby taste?'

'Basil—it really makes the dish, doesn't it?'

'I knew *you'd* know what it was.' He was almost triumphant, and she felt another twinge of uncertainty. Was he hinting that she should concentrate on the domestic scene rather than her career? Or had he a passion for home comforts and thought she might be just the person to provide them?

When they had both cleared their plates he asked, 'Dessert? Coffee?'

'Just coffee, I think. What about you?'

'No dessert for me either.'

'You're welcome to come back to the cottage for coffee. Then I can let Jenny get home at a reasonable hour.'

She wasn't at all sure if she was wise to make the offer, but she felt she owed it to him after he'd treated her to the show and the meal.

'That sounds good.'

He settled the bill and found a cab to drive them the short distance to her cottage.

'Not a peep from her,' Jenny greeted them.

Brian arrived at almost the same moment to collect his wife.

'Come in and we'll have coffee together,' Jenny invited eagerly.

Brian shook his head. 'I think it's late enough. We'll get on home, if you don't mind.'

Fran closed the door behind them. 'Take a seat. I'll make the coffee this time.' She made the joky reference to Cal's earlier visit in an attempt to lower the sexual tension she sensed building between them.

He nodded his agreement, but followed her into the kitchen and watched her set the coffee-maker in action.

She set out two mugs on a tray, together with sugar and milk. 'Sorry, no cream.'

'You don't spoil yourself very often, do you? That's why I've brought you this.'

He took a gift-wrapped parcel from his jacket pocket and handed it to her. 'A CD to add to your collection. It features the company we saw so I bought a copy when I collected the tickets. Now you'll be able to listen to your hero to your heart's content.'

She coloured again. 'You shouldn't have done that, not after taking me to the show.'

'Why not? Everyone deserves a treat occasionally.'

'I know, but...'

'But what?'

'Well, you've given me enough this evening.'

'I've enjoyed it, too, you know.'

She was about to nod her agreement when he moved closer and captured her head between his hands. Then he gently kissed her lips.

Startled, Fran tried to pull away but she was trapped. 'I've wanted to sample those lips since the day we met, and they certainly fulfil their promise.'

He lowered his lips to hers again. They were warm, and firm, and dry. Freed by the belief that it wasn't just a thank-you-for-your-company kiss, this time her lips parted and their tongues meshed in a sudden frenzy of desire.

He groaned and moved away, holding her at arm's length.

Fran pulled herself free of his grasp and told him shakily, 'I—I'd better pour the coffee.'

'Coffee has suddenly lost its attraction. I was just wondering why I hadn't done that long ago,' he murmured, pulling her into his arms again. When he eventually released her he murmured shakily, 'I think we need to talk, Fran.'

Panic and excitement in equal amounts churned inside her. She wanted to hear what he was about to say, but she knew so little about him that she was afraid in case it destroyed her hopes for ever.

'We do?' Her words were drowned by a piercing wail from upstairs.

Fran raced upstairs and it was quite a time before she came down the stairs, cradling a sobbing Naomi. 'I'm sorry, Cal. She's not usually like this. I don't know what's the matter so I think it'll be best if you go and I stay upstairs with her. You can call a cab from here.'

'Is there anything I can do? Is she ill?'

Fran shook her head. 'I don't think so, thanks. I do apologise for throwing you out, especially after you've given me such a pleasant evening.'

He raised a rueful eyebrow. 'Not to worry, and I won't bother with a cab. The walk'll clear my head. I'll see myself out.'

'Thanks again, Cal. For everything.'

His gaze lingered on them both before he nodded and came over to kiss Fran lightly on the cheek. At his approach Naomi screamed louder than ever so, raising his eyebrows apologetically, he lifted a hand in farewell and was gone. Fran bolted the door behind him and climbed sadly up the stairs.

As she tried to soothe her fractious daughter her thoughts were anything but calm. Her body was still tingling with increased awareness of him and she wondered what he might have told her and what might have happened if it hadn't been for Naomi.

Naomi! The thought of her daughter dashed her euphoria. Would Naomi cause a problem between them? Sure, he was always considerate and appeared interested in her welfare, but was that just the way he was with everyone?

Naomi didn't settle until well into the early hours, and Fran was grateful that she could sleep in late the next morning. When Naomi eventually awoke it was obvious to Fran that she had been sickening for something the night before. She was hot and sticky and extremely fretful.

She rang Jenny. 'We won't be able to come shopping with you as planned. Naomi is feverish so I think it's better if we stay indoors today.'

Jenny commiserated, and offered to get any shopping Fran required.

'The only necessity is nappies.'

'I'll get those. If you don't need them today you can collect them tomorrow. Don't worry about the money at the moment.'

'You'll probably need them before me,' Fran said with

a laugh. 'We'll be round tomorrow morning early, all being well.'

'Great. I can't wait to hear all about your evening. See you tomorrow.'

'Nothing to tell,' Fran said, and thoughtfully replaced the receiver, conscious that nothing at all had been changed by their evening out. Thanks to Naomi.

By Wednesday evening, the little girl seemed much better and even settled early so Fran had a longer than usual evening to do many of the tasks she'd been putting off for days. Her peace was shattered by her telephone ringing well after nine.

'Hi.' It was Cal. 'I wondered how Naomi is.'

Her heart leaping uncontrollably, Fran had to struggle to answer in an even tone. 'She's sleeping, thanks, Cal. Her temperature was raised this morning, but she seems much better again this evening. Probably teething.'

'Would you like me to come round?'

Although there was nothing she would have liked better, Fran was worried that Naomi might wake again and that a repeat performance might turn Cal against her daughter. She hastily refused his offer. 'I didn't get much sleep last night and I'm on an early tomorrow so I'm just on my way to bed. I'll no doubt see you in the morning.'

'Oh! OK! I'll look forward to that.' Fran hoped it *was* disappointment and not relief she could hear in his voice. 'I'm glad she's better.'

'Have you had a busy day?'

'Afraid so. It doesn't look like it's getting any easier so you'd better get that good night's sleep you plan. Goodnight, Fran.'

Although Fran spent a restless night, Naomi slept right through. When eating her breakfast, she seemed back to her normal self so Fran was reasonably happy to leave her with Jenny.

On her way to the unit she was apprehensive about meeting up with Cal again for although their outing on Tuesday had proved they had so much in common it had left so many questions unanswered.

The day was so hectic, though, that Fran hardly saw Cal, and certainly not to speak to alone, so when she handed over to the afternoon shift at three she left the unit reluctantly.

She was pleased to discover, however, that her daughter seemed back to normal. She took her straight home, hoping that perhaps Cal would ring again and suggest a visit. This evening she would welcome him.

When the telephone remained stubbornly silent she thought about ringing and inviting him round, but realised she had no idea where to find him if he wasn't at the hospital.

The thought was sobering. Perhaps he didn't want her to know anything about his private life. Perhaps she hadn't been asking the right questions or he had been deliberately evasive. Perhaps a commitment elsewhere was what he'd been about to tell her.

He seemed to know everything about her and yet she knew so little about him, apart from his outburst about females when she hadn't wanted to testify.

She had gathered that day that he'd had an unhappy relationship, but it hadn't been mentioned since and so she hadn't felt able to broach the subject again.

Friday morning was bright so Fran took Naomi into the park again, and this time took some bread with them to feed the ducks. A peaceful morning was what she needed, before facing the afternoon shift.

She was relieved to discover that, despite Cal's prediction on Wednesday evening, the unit had quietened right down and was relatively peaceful by the time she arrived on duty. During the afternoon she even found the time to make him a cup of tea.

'All well in the nursery now?'

'Fine, thanks.' Still unsure of him, her response was guarded.

'Are you working all weekend?'

'Afraid so. An early tomorrow and a late Sunday. What about you?'

'No peace for me either. I'm on call for the whole unit. Male and female.'

'I'll try not to disturb you too often.'

He laughed. 'Pity.'

'I promise I'll keep the coffee-machine primed.'

'That's my girl.'

She refilled the cup he'd just drained.

'We're on take for emergencies all weekend so, if there's nothing pressing, I think I'll seize the opportunity to sneak away.'

Hoping to discover more about him, Fran asked, 'Can you be reached on your bleeper at home?'

'I can, but I also have an on-call room in the hospital.'

His reply told her nothing, except that he couldn't live too far from the site.

He left the unit soon afterwards, and though Fran knew he would be available if needed she felt the now familiar sense of loss at his departure and a sense of doom at his reluctance to say anything more about his living arrangements.

CHAPTER SIX

FRAN had just completed serving the patients' suppers when the telephone rang. When she lifted the receiver the accident and emergency clerk said, 'We have an admission for you. You do still have a bed, do you?'

'Yes.'

'That's good because she's already on her way over there. Dr Ward is with her and will give you all the details.'

Fran and Allie had the bed ready by the time Rob and a staff nurse arrived with the patient. They made her comfortable and Rob checked that the intravenous infusion was running satisfactorily, before indicating that Fran should follow him into the centre of the ward.

'I'm pretty sure she's a candidate for a pacemaker but I thought we were losing her so I bleeped Cal and the cardiac team. They are both on their way.'

'What's her name?'

'Betty Mead. Apart from her address, that's all we know about her. All we can do is keep an eye on her obs until he arrives.'

As they returned to the bed space Allie looked up. 'She's arresting.'

Rob started external cardiac massage while Fran pushed the cardiac emergency button to alert the crash team.

The moment they ran into the ward Rob urged, 'Hurry.'

Fran took over the job of breathing for the patient via a mask and hand-operated bag that maintained a regular oxygen supply. The defibrillation machine was moved speedily into position and Allie plugged it in. The members of the crash team attached the leads from the machine to the patient's chest, and adjusted the read-out so that Rob could see it. The paddles were quickly positioned on the patient's chest.

'Two hundred joules, please,' Rob ordered.

The technician nodded. 'Stand clear.'

'We'll get more oxygen into her with a tube.'

Deftly removing the mask, the anaesthetist, who had arrived in answer to Fran's summons, speedily slid a tube into Betty's trachea and reattached the oxygen, barely disrupting the supply to the patient.

'No response,' Rob told them. 'Repeat the shock—200 joules again. Stand clear, everybody.'

This time Fran saw a definite improvement in the trace on the cardiac monitor.

'I can just feel a pulse.'

In all the confusion the details surrounding the patient's admission and diagnosis were not discussed, but before the staff nurse from Accident and Emergency left them to it Fran was sure she heard the girl mention Dr Jenner's name to Rob.

When Cal arrived, Rob described his findings and his actions. 'When I first saw her the pulse rate was below forty. I requested a full blood count and clotting screen and have alerted the cardiac team. Should I start antibiotic cover or wait for the experts?'

'Get on with it, Rob. She clearly needs a pacemaker and the sooner the better.'

When the team of experts arrived they agreed with the diagnosis, and after further tests arranged for a pacemaker to be inserted under a local anaesthetic.

Much later, when the patient's condition was stabilising, her neighbour arrived. 'I couldn't help wondering how she is so I got my son to run me up here. I was so worried when her GP didn't show up. It seemed such a long time. I guess he must have been busy.'

'You called the doctor?'

The neighbour nodded. 'Betty keeps his number by the

telephone. I rang, and said I thought it was urgent, but when he didn't come I panicked and called the ambulance.'

'She's a lot to be grateful to you for. What's her doctor's name?'

'I'm not sure. Her usual doctor has been ill for some time.'

Fran was thoughtful as she left Allie and Rob to tell her what was happening and to try and glean what other information they could about Betty Mead.

As she returned to check Betty's condition Fran's curiosity was roused by what the neighbour had said.

The whole episode was so frighteningly reminiscent of Mrs Dubarry's admission that when she had a few spare moments, just before going off duty, she checked what information they had on Betty's notes. The GP's name was given as Dr Purdy.

'Rob?' she queried hesitantly as the junior doctor came into the office to collect some papers. 'Did you hear someone say Dr Jenner was her doctor?'

Rob frowned. 'Dr Purdy's her GP. I remember that because it's almost the only info we had about her.'

'Yes, I know that, but I thought I heard the staff nurse who brought her from A and E mention Dr Jenner to you.'

'I don't remember, but that's not to say she didn't. We had a rather hairy few moments so I probably wouldn't even have heard the Angel Gabriel's trumpet.'

Fran laughed. 'I didn't hear that either.'

'Thank goodness for that! If you had I'd be seriously worried!'

'All the same, I think I'll see if I can find out if I did hear her say something about him.'

Rob had opened the office door as she spoke but he turned and said, 'I should forget the man, Fran. Dr Jenner is not worth wasting your time on.'

Fran tried to do just that. When she found that the casualty nurse was already off duty and not expected back until Monday evening she tried to convince herself that she had been mistaken and that the similarity to Mrs Dubarry's admission was causing her imagination to work overtime. Even if Mrs Mead's doctor was called Jenner, it was stretching coincidence far too far for it to be the same doctor who'd been the hospital locum.

Despite her resolve, she didn't sleep well that night either. Memories of the threats to Naomi returned to plague her, undermining her confidence that she had heard the last of Dr Jenner.

It was all she could do the next morning to drag herself round to Jenny's with Naomi. She didn't want to leave her for a moment, but she knew she had to learn to trust somebody other than herself and, as it was Saturday, Brian would be there with Jenny.

When she finally arrived on duty she was relieved to discover that Betty Mead's condition was gradually improving. Perhaps now she could find out the truth. Soon, however, Fran was too busy to worry about her own problems, and as he was on call for the whole unit she saw little of Cal.

When he did come to check on her patients, and she offered him a quick cup of coffee, she sensed Cal watching her thoughtfully.

'Everything all right?' she asked.

'I'm not sure,' he responded suspiciously. 'Until you tell me why you and Rob were discussing Dr Jenner last night?'

Her heart plummeting, Fran closed her eyes in despair. All her hard work to prove herself to him counted for nothing as she realised they were back at square one. How on earth did he know? Had Rob told him or had he been eavesdropping again?

'Dr Jenner?' she prevaricated, trying to discover how much he knew.

'Yes. I rather gathered Rob was advising you to forget the man.' His tone contained more than a hint of distrust.

'Rather surprising, considering you assured me you didn't know him.'

'I...er...Rob, well, Rob realised that I was uneasy because the circumstances of Mrs Mead's admission mirrored what had happened on my first evening shift.'

'And?'

Fran felt the depth of his disapproval keenly. 'That was all.'

'I wonder—the same as I'm beginning to wonder if you've ever told me the whole truth.'

Fran was outraged. 'If you don't believe me, why don't you ask Rob?'

He closed the office door and grasped her shoulders firmly, forcing her round to meet his gaze. 'Because I'd rather hear the truth from you,' he told her quietly. Fran tried ineffectually to escape his hold.

'You've already heard it. You obviously didn't recognise it—or at least believe it. Now release me, please.'

Disappointment at his returning distrust made her speak more sharply than she'd intended. Fran tried to soften the harshness. 'I do have patients to see to, you know.'

No sooner had the words left her lips than Cal did as she asked. So speedily that it was almost an insult, he allowed her to move away into the ward—and how she wished he hadn't!

As she carried out her duties she found it difficult to keep her thoughts from wandering. She knew it wasn't the moment to try and convince him, but would she ever find the right time?

There seemed a certain inevitability about what was happening. However hard she tried to rebuild her life, someone or something was going to prevent her from succeeding.

'You look tired, Nurse. Something wrong?' Mrs Jenkins greeted her when she made her way into the day room.

Fran smiled and shook her head. 'I'm ready for a day

off, but as I asked for next weekend off I have a little longer to wait.'

'Doing something special, are you?'

Fran shook her head. 'I was looking forward to seeing my parents. They're living abroad and were coming home to see me.'

'Were?'

'Yep. Their flight was cancelled and they're not arriving until next Wednesday now.'

'We'll have to find you something else to do, then!'

Fran laughed. 'Believe me, by Friday all I'll want to do is to collapse in front of the television with my daughter.'

'How old is she?'

'Seven months.'

'Lovely age. Does her dad see to her when you're in here?'

Fran shook her head. 'He died before she was born.'

'Oh, I'm sorry, love. Me and my big mouth.'

Fran gave her a reassuring smile. 'You weren't to know and I've come to terms with it now.'

When, some time later, she returned to the office to collect some notes she was disappointed to find it empty, even though she had dreaded coming face to face with Cal. For the remainder of her shift he was supposedly busy in other parts of the hospital. Whether on genuine business or not, Fran was unsure, but as she had no emergencies on her side of the unit she had no reason to call him.

She collected Naomi and returned home with a heavy heart. 'So much for our relationship developing further,' she told Naomi, kissing her on the cheek. 'Perhaps you have better judgement than I do, sweetheart. If you hadn't woken on Tuesday night, goodness knows what might have happened. And I guess I wouldn't be feeling too happy about it right now, would I?'

Naomi didn't answer, merely grabbed a fistful of Fran's hair and drew it towards her mouth.

'Oh, no, you don't, you little rascal. You might know men better than I do, but there's some things you're not going to get away with.'

On Sunday Cal treated her as if she were nothing more than a casual colleague. During the couple of times she had to contact him about patients he discussed business and nothing more.

When Fran reported for her Monday early shift, she was pleased to discover Betty feeling much better and eager to chat. When she had visited all of her other patients, and supplied all their wants and needs, Fran took the opportunity to ask Betty if she remembered exactly what had happened to her.

'I can't tell you anything about Friday night, love, but I've had similar attacks on and off for weeks, though I suppose this one was worse than they've been before.'

'What did Dr Purdy say about them?'

'He said they were caused by my heart slowing. He said he'd refer me to a specialist, but he's been away ill for a few weeks and a lovely chap has taken his place. Dr Jenner. Do you know him?'

Betty's words sent Fran's hopes that she'd been wrong spinning out of control. Wanting to be absolutely certain she had the name right, she said, 'Dr Jenner, you say.'

'That's right. He's wonderful. I've never met such a caring doctor. In fact, I've grown so fond of him that as I've no family of my own I've made a will in his favour.'

Her heart plummeted. Fran had to struggle to acknowledge the information with a smile, but as soon as she could escape, without Betty thinking her rude, she made her way to the office to think, uninterrupted.

If this Dr Jenner was the same one who had worked at the hospital, had he deliberately not turned up when Mrs Mead needed him because he knew about the change to her will and wanted her to die?

Fran closed her eyes in dismay as another and much

more disturbing thought occurred to her. Mrs Dubarry had had no family either! Had Dr Jenner somehow persuaded *her* to change her will as well? Was that why he hadn't responded to Fran's repeated calls?

If so, how many others had he neglected in the same way? She groaned miserably. By not telling anybody about the threats to her daughter, had she condemned others to his evil ministrations?

If Cal or the hospital medical personnel officer had had even the faintest inkling that there could have been a problem, a thorough investigation would have been carried out and Dr Jenner would probably have been found out. However, to safeguard her daughter she had selfishly kept quiet about the threatening notes she had received.

She wasn't fit to be a nurse. And yet there was no way she could have suspected the truth. Knowing he wouldn't be employed at the hospital again, she'd closed her mind to what might happen in his next post. If she'd thought about it at all, it had been to persuade herself that he'd probably learnt his lesson and would be more conscientious in future.

She was still sitting with her head resting on her hands when Cal came to see his patients. 'Looks like you've plenty of time for a quick ward round.' His tone was almost scathing.

As she lifted her head he took one look at her face and closed the office door. 'What on earth's the matter?'

When she didn't answer he said encouragingly, 'Is it Naomi?'

Fran shook her head. 'Not really.'

'What is it?' He moved round to her side of the desk and placed an arm lightly round her shoulder. 'You look as if you've seen a ghost.'

'I—I— It…' She couldn't get the words out. She didn't know how to explain, or even if she wanted to, because one thing was certain—if she told him what she now believed, Naomi's life was going to be in much greater danger than it had been before.

Cal was clearly anxious. 'Is it a problem on the ward?'

Fran shook her head, but said, 'Yes and no.'

'You're talking in riddles, Fran. Would a coffee help?'

She nodded. While he was finding one for her perhaps she could work out what she ought to do. For Naomi's sake she wanted to keep quiet, but she realised she could do so no longer if she was ever to live with herself comfortably.

Cal returned with two mugs on a tray. He closed the door again and pulled his chair close to hers.

When she'd taken a couple of sips he urged. 'Now, tell me what the problem is.'

'I'm so ashamed, Cal. I think it's because of my cowardice that Mrs Mead nearly died. If it hadn't been for her neighbour...'

Cal shook his head as he tried to understand. 'What on earth are you talking about, Fran? How can it be your fault?'

'Because, because— Oh! I don't know what to do. If I should be telling you this.' Tears were streaming down her cheeks, and Cal took a tissue from the box on the desk and gently wiped them away.

'Fran, love...' he rested a hand gently on her arm '...you're not making any sense. Why not drink your coffee, take a deep breath and start at the very beginning?'

Her nerve endings shredded by his touch—and even more by him calling her 'love'—she did as he said and then murmured, 'I've been such a fool, Cal. When I first started here, you remember Dr Jenner didn't put in an appearance when he was called to a new admission.'

'I remember it well.' Clearly puzzled, he was frowning at her now. 'Especially as I couldn't understand why you were suddenly so reluctant to assist any investigation into what happened.'

'I was furious with him at the time but...but then...'

Fran pursed her lips miserably and shook her head, before continuing. 'I found notes under my windscreen-wiper—threatening Naomi if I talked about it. I tried to dismiss them as a practical joke.'

Horrified, Cal moved away from her. 'And you didn't think it was important enough to tell anyone?'

'How could I, Cal? The note threatened Naomi if I did. I didn't know who to turn to or what to do. I guessed it meant he'd done something wrong, but I thought it was probably something minor and I couldn't put her at risk for that, could I?'

Cal was shaking his head slowly. 'You thought someone would go to those lengths for ''something minor''. I can't believe I'm hearing this. If you'd only told me. I could have—'

'I...I'd only just met you... I couldn't take the risk. I was terrified that once you knew you'd feel you had to do something about it and now...' A broken sob escaped her lips. 'And now it seems I've put the lives of others in danger, by saying nothing.'

He stifled her protest with a raised hand and murmured, 'I suppose I can understand why you felt you couldn't, but I don't see where Mrs Mead comes in. How could your actions possibly affect her?'

'You asked why Rob and I were discussing Dr Jenner on Friday night.'

'Yes.'

'Well...I thought I'd heard the Accident and Emergency nurse mention the name, but when I checked with Rob he was sure I was imagining things.'

'Why didn't you ask the nurse?'

'There was so much to be done that I didn't have a moment until later. By that time she'd gone off duty and would not be back until this evening when she starts her stint of nights.'

Cal frowned, his disappointment at her behaviour scything through her like a knife. 'I still don't see why you think you've put other lives at risk.'

'Mrs Mead. Her GP is ill and she's been seen recently by a locum.' She sighed deeply and tried to bite back her tears. 'The locum was called Jenner. I know I may be putting two and two together and making five—and I hope I am,' she wailed hysterically, 'but somehow, after what Mrs Mead has just told me, I don't think so.'

'Why?'

'As she has no family she has changed her will in Dr Jenner's favour. She thinks he's absolutely wonderful, but I—I think very differently. He didn't turn up when he was called on Friday, and if she'd died he'd have inherited everything.'

The awful significance of what she was saying rendered Cal speechless.

'And if you remember,' Fran knew she couldn't hide the truth any longer, 'Mrs Dubarry had no family either. It would be interesting to see who got her money.'

'I can't believe anyone— I—I couldn't understand why you changed your mind about giving evidence to an enquiry but never in my wildest dreams could I have envisaged anything so—so—'

Furious now, Fran interrupted his harangue. 'I didn't know any of this then. I just thought he'd been missing from the hospital when he should have been on call, or something similar.'

'I don't consider that minor. I still can't believe you allowed him to get away with the threats. It was nothing less than blackmail and that's a criminal offence. How *could* you keep quiet about a doctor behaving in that way?'

'If I'd had any idea of the extent of his wrongdoing, I'd have been the first to stop him. But I didn't.'

'And left other patients to suffer.'

Fran whispered miserably, 'I knew you wouldn't understand, and you don't, do you? I really thought the note was just to frighten me into silence. I didn't think of it as black-mail and then when the enquiry was dropped and you told me that he wouldn't be employed here again and I didn't hear anything more—'

'Did you tell Jenny about the threatening notes?'

'No. I—'

'I wasn't the only one kept in the dark, then.'

'It was my problem and I had to work it out in my own way.'

He rubbed his cheek ruefully. 'I'm as much to blame in some ways. I knew something wasn't right. I should have questioned you further. I thought you were probably cov-ering up for Dr Jenner, which, of course, you were, but not for the reasons I suspected.'

Fran looked up at him with reproach in her eyes. 'I guessed as much. When you came to the cottage to tell me the post-mortem had revealed that Mrs Dubarry's death had been due to natural causes, you came to check up on me, didn't you?'

When Cal didn't answer immediately she murmured, 'I knew what you were thinking, and I was glad I could prove you wrong. You've never really trusted me, have you?'

Cal ignored her outburst.

'We obviously can't keep this to ourselves now. If you're right, others could already be in danger. Before I do any-thing, though, you need to warn Jenny and tell her the whole truth.'

'I expect I'll lose my job anyway so it's probably better if I resign and look after Naomi myself.'

Her statement clearly startled him. 'Why should you have to leave? OK, you may be reprimanded for an error of judgement, but I think the powers that be will understand why you didn't say anything.'

'Does that mean, well, that *you* understand why I did it?' His disappointment in her had left Fran feeling more acutely alone than she'd felt all through her pregnancy and Naomi's birth.

'I do wish you'd confided in me. I'm not so unapproachable, am I?'

'You didn't trust me when we first met, did you? And you were quick enough to believe I was shacked up with Dr Jenner!'

'I think that's a little unfair of you, Fran. To my mind, you became a different person in just twenty-four hours. I wanted to discover what had happened to change you so rapidly from the lively and open colleague I thought I'd met on that first day to a patently scared nurse who avoided answering my questions.'

Unable to bear the disillusionment she could read in his eyes, she lowered her gaze. She had worked hard to regain his respect and had thought she was winning. Until today. Now he was clearly so unforgiving of her behaviour that she had no hope of ever doing so again.

She sighed deeply. 'I can't sit here any longer. I must see if I'm needed.'

'You can't run away from this, Fran.'

'I'm not. I just feel so helpless.' Fran didn't try to hide her misery. 'I'll contact Medical Personnel with all the details and give up my post here with effect from tomorrow.'

'There'll be no need for that,' Cal told her sharply. 'Even if what you've told me turns out to be true it's not your fault.'

'I know I can't be blamed for what Dr Jenner has done, but keeping what I did know about him to myself was hardly the action of a responsible member of the nursing staff, was it?' Conscious of tears pricking her eyelids, she turned away.

He took both her hands in his. 'Calm down, Fran. I think you're being too hard on yourself now. Look, will you promise to leave this with me and not make any rash decisions until I get back to you?'

'I can't risk Naomi—'

'There should be no threat to Naomi until we make a move to inform the authorities. In the meantime, I'll try and work out a plan of action. You're a good nurse, something we're not exactly overstocked with here. The last thing you should do is resign over something beyond your control.'

Any pleasure she might have experienced at his compliment was destroyed by her anxiety over Naomi. She chewed her bottom lip anxiously. 'You promise you'll let me know before you take any official action?'

'Of course.'

At the end of her shift Fran made her way to Jenny's house with a heavy heart. She didn't want to worry her friend, and as there should be no threat for the next twenty-four hours she merely told her that after Tuesday she would probably be taking a few days off work.

Jenny walked with her to the door. 'Are you finding it too much, working and coping with Naomi?'

'Not really, but there are a few problems I need to sort out.'

Jenny frowned. 'You weren't cross because I let Cal take Naomi on Saturday?'

Fran turned and hugged her friend. 'No. Of course not. I think I might have to look for another job, though. Perhaps one with more regular hours.'

'The hours are no problem as far as I'm concerned—'

'I know that. Jenny,' Fran broke in impatiently, then, seeing the crestfallen look on her friend's face, murmured, 'Sorry, Jen, I'm probably over-tired at the moment. Everything will look different tomorrow.'

Fran returned to her cottage, feeling more dejected than ever. Not only had she alienated Cal but she had upset Jenny. And after she had been so good to her. She sighed deeply. Life wasn't making things at all easy for her.

Before settling Naomi to kick on a rug on the floor, she

cuddled her and kissed her cheek. 'If I have to stay home with you, sweetheart, it'll be a bonus. We'll manage somehow.'

She made herself a cup of coffee and settled down to try and figure out where she could make cuts in her budget and to discover if there was any kind of work she could do from home.

She hadn't got very far when Jenny rang. 'Are you OK, Fran?'

'I'm fine.'

'Fran, if it's a cash flow problem I don't mind not being paid for the time being.'

'Thanks, Jenny. You're a true friend. I only wish money was the problem, but it's not. As I said, it's something I've got to work out for myself. I'll see you tomorrow.' Fran could say no more because tears were welling up in her eyes. Jenny was the best thing that had happened to her in this nightmare year.

The next afternoon Cal appeared in the unit almost before Fran had finished taking the hand-over report. When she had detailed the duties to be done by the two care assistants he closed the door behind them.

'I've given the problem a lot of thought. Before I say anything about this to Medical Personnel I'm going to try and discover the contents of Mrs Dubarry's will. If it's what you suspect, this isn't a matter for the hospital. It's a matter for the police.'

Fran was apprehensive. 'What are you going to do?'

'It's probably too early for the will to have been proved so I'll see what I can find out from her neighbours. Also, I intend checking whether the details Mrs Mead's general practice were given about their Dr Jenner tally with the CV Medical Personnel here holds.'

Fran rested her head in her hands. 'Do you think that's wise, Cal? Wouldn't it be better to leave it to the police?'

'I'm being very careful, I promise. The last thing we want is to let Jenner know someone's onto him. If the police are involved, he's sure to find out.'

'I know, but—'

'I'd like to find out about Mrs Dubarry's will first.'

'The man who made the threats knows about Naomi being left with Jenny, knew my car and where exactly to find it and, no doubt, knows where I live. Goodness knows how he found out all the information.'

'The same way as I found out your address that night I called to see you were OK after you fainted.'

'Which was?'

'You filled in a personal status form on your return from maternity leave, didn't you?'

'Yes.'

'Instead of next of kin you gave Jenny as your daughter's carer.'

'But how—? Surely the form is confidential?'

'The information has to be available in case anything happens to you out of office hours so it's entered on the computer.'

Fran was horrified. 'You mean anyone can locate information about every member of staff?'

'Only nursing officers and medical staff have access to that particular file.'

'Only!'

Cal rested a hand on her arm. 'Calm down. After this, I intend demanding that the system is changed.'

Fran shook her head miserably. 'Under the circumstances, I feel pretty vulnerable, staying where he knows he can find me. He knows my movements. I think perhaps I ought to take Naomi right away where we can't be found.'

'Where would you go? Abroad to your parents?'

She shook her head. 'I haven't told them about Naomi yet.'

His eyes widened in surprise. 'Don't you think you ought to?'

She shrugged. 'They're coming home on sabbatical soon and I was going to do it then. I thought it would be easier face to face.'

'Have you any other relative or a friend you could stay with?'

Fran shook her head. 'Not that I can think of. I can't involve Jenny. Looking after Naomi is supposed to be therapy for her—they're trying desperately for a baby. The last thing she needs is to be scared out of her wits so I've told her that today is Naomi's last day with her for the time being.

'I'm frightened, Cal. Not for myself, but for Naomi. At least if the police knew they would be able to protect us.'

Cal sighed. 'I shouldn't be too sure about that. However, I can.'

A frown creased her forehead. 'How? You're—'

'Hear me out, Fran, and don't fly off the handle, please. If I start making waves, you are extremely vulnerable in that isolated cottage on your own.'

'You don't need to tell me—'

'Let me finish. I think it would be a good idea if you had someone living in the cottage with you. If you agree, I'm prepared to move in until this is sorted out.'

Her heart pounding, Fran turned to him with wide eyes. 'Move in? You don't have to do that. We'll be all right.'

He said quietly, 'I know I don't *have* to,' then added, 'You know, I rather fancy myself as a bodyguard.'

When Fran remained pensive he continued, 'After all, if I go to the police with our suspicions, it'll be my actions that will put Naomi's life in danger and so it's only fair.'

She felt a perverse surge of disappointment that that was the only reason for his suggestion but she was, nevertheless, grateful.

'After all, this was thrust upon you through no fault of your own.'

Fran looked at him, still wide-eyed. It sounded a wonderful idea to her, but what about him? His private life was still a mystery to her, but surely he couldn't just opt out of his present commitments? Eventually she struggled to swallow the lump that was threatening to block her throat. 'I— I can't expect you to disrupt your life for me.'

'Why ever not?'

'It'll ruin your social life and...and...' Fran's voice trailed off before she said something she might regret.

'And?'

'What about when you're on call?'

'I've thought about that. Pam Wood is always complaining I don't take enough time off. I should be able to rearrange the rota for the short time necessary.'

Fran's heart missed a beat. A short time. Was that all it would be? Despite her half-hearted protests, she knew there was nothing she would like better, but if she allowed him into her home she knew she would hate the subsequent loneliness even more when the matter was resolved and he moved out again.

'Well, do you think it's a good idea?'

Fran nodded. 'Perhaps...'

Cal sighed with exasperation. 'I thought you might welcome me with open arms!'

Unsure how to take his remark, Fran smiled nervously. 'I must say I haven't enjoyed arriving home in the dark recently, and I'm still positively jumpy if someone comes calling late at night.'

'Why haven't you said something before?'

'Because it's my life and my problem.'

'Aren't you forgetting Naomi?'

'She's my responsibility.'

He searched her face with lingering disbelief. 'I thought

we were friends. Surely it's the place of friends to offer help when necessary.'

'I hardly know you.'

'And you don't trust anyone, do you?'

'Would you, after what life has dumped on me recently?'

When he didn't immediately answer, but shook his head in despair, she murmured, 'No, I'm wrong. I wouldn't be without Naomi. She brings me so much happiness—and heartache at the moment.'

'So, will you let me help protect her?' he asked eagerly.

'If you really don't mind.' She laughed. 'I do feel vulnerable and so perhaps, after all, I'll welcome you with open arms. But I warn you. You're in for some disturbed nights.'

CHAPTER SEVEN

FRAN saw Cal's eyes light up with amusement as he said teasingly, 'I'll look forward to it.'

Recognising his meaning, she said firmly, 'It'll be Naomi that disturbs you, not me.'

He pretended to be disappointed. 'Ah, well, can't have everything, I suppose.'

Despite his macho bravado, Fran was aware that he was offering nothing more than to take care of Naomi and herself—and that only for the short time it would take to nail Dr Jenner. She mustn't read more into his actions than he intended.

'OK. I'll speak to Pam, and if it's OK I'll bring a few necessities along when I finish here.'

She offered hesitantly, 'I'll find something for us to eat once Naomi's settled, shall I?'

'Hey, I'm not out to make extra work for you. I can look after myself. My pasta bakes are amazing.'

'I don't doubt it, but you can't live on pasta. Can you?'

He grinned. 'Perhaps you're about to find out.'

His words sent a tingle of anticipation scurrying the length of her spine. Was this an indication that he usually did his own cooking?

She decided the ward office was not the place to try and find out. 'I'll see you some time this evening, then. And although I'll feed you, I'm not setting a precedent. OK?'

He appeared momentarily taken aback by her vehemence, but quickly recovered his equilibrium.

'And now can I ask you about Mrs Dunn?'

'Last evening's admission with query post viral syndrome?'

Fran nodded.

'What's the problem?'

'She's none too special today and I feel something is going on that we aren't aware of. She's another of Dr Purdy's patients—'

'You mean she could be another of Dr Jenner's victims?'

'Not exactly. She has been admitted in what seems like good time. It's just that under the circumstances...'

'I think I know what you mean.'

He took a look at the patient's blood test results taken the day before. 'She's certainly anaemic. Let's go and take another look at her, and then do a quick round of the other patients.'

They made their way to the bedside of the elderly lady. 'Hello, Mrs Dunn. How're you doing?'

When she wearily nodded that she was fine Cal asked, 'Were you up and about this morning?'

'Only for a short time. I got so breathless.'

'How long have you been feeling like this?'

'It's hard to say. At first I thought the tiredness was old age. Then I kept waking up soaked with perspiration. Even when it was so cold and I was losing weight.'

He motioned to Fran to draw the bed curtains. 'Let's take a look at you. I'd like to listen to your chest and feel your tummy.'

While Mrs Dunn organised herself Cal studied her charts and frowned. 'She's had a low grade pyrexia since she was admitted as well,' he murmured to Fran.

'Sorry to be so slow, Doctor. I'm so weak these days that everything takes me twice as long.'

Cal's frown increased as he listened to her heart. 'When did you last go to the dentist, Mrs Dunn?'

'The dentist?' His patient was astounded by his question. 'I haven't a clue—it must be some time last year.'

'You still have some of your own teeth?'

She nodded. 'So say, but they're nearly all filling.'

'Slide down the bed a little way and let me feel your tum.' As she did so he asked, 'Did the dentist know you were taking tablets for high blood pressure?'

'I shouldn't think so for a moment.'

Cal palpated the left side of her abdomen then, covering her up, indicated that he had finished his examination. 'I think I'd like some more blood tests, Mrs Dunn. I'll go and organise them now.'

Having made her patient comfortable, Fran joined him in the office.

'Sub-acutte bacterial endocarditis?' she queried.

'Her symptoms are almost too classic, but the more I think about it the more sure I am. If her blood pressure has been high enough, it could well have damaged some of her heart valves, allowing the infection from any dental lesions to spread.

'I'm requesting immediate blood cultures and will start her on IV antibiotics. She's already been down for a chest X-ray, hasn't she?'

When he'd done all he could for the time being he told Fran that he was going to see Pam Wood and then see what he could find out about Mrs Dubarry and Dr Jenner.

Fran didn't see him for the remainder of her shift and she left to collect Naomi, without knowing if Pam had agreed to his plans and what, if anything, he had found out. And as she made her way to Jenny's house she couldn't help wondering if he would turn up as planned and, more important, would he try to cross the boundaries they had set?

Despite not knowing the answers, she quickly cleared junk out of her small bedroom, moved Naomi into her own room and made up the bed for him.

She then searched out the ingredients for a tasty evening meal and finally decided on a simple fish pie.

Her preparations were well under way by ten-thirty, but there was still no sign of Cal or word from him. Convinced that she'd been let down again, she sighed deeply. He'd made the suggestion on the spur of the moment and had regretted it later.

She had been a fool to expect anything else. She'd set out on this journey alone and that was the way it would continue. It was clearly her fate never to meet a man who didn't have a hidden agenda—someone who, for some reason, found it easier to distrust than trust her.

It was past eleven when Cal eventually put in an appearance, an overnight bag slung over his shoulder.

She had long since eaten her own meal and turned off the oven.

'I'm sorry, Fran. I was unavoidably delayed.'

'Thanks for letting me know.'

'I tried, but your phone is out of order. I've reported it.'

Her eyes wild, Fran raced across to lift up the receiver. 'It's dead,' she confirmed. 'Oh, Cal, do you think it's been deliberately cut?'

He moved across the room and removed the receiver from her hand. 'Who on earth by?'

'Well, Dr Jenner, of course.'

He shook his head and, taking her arm, led her across to the settee, and settled beside her. 'You're getting paranoid now, Fran. He can't possibly know that anyone suspects him at the moment.'

'We can't be sure of that. And the telephone was OK yesterday.'

'It may have escaped your notice, but we had quite a gale last night. When I reported the fault they said they've been inundated with calls about lines brought down in the night. With the number of trees around this house, it's more than likely a branch has severed your line.'

'I wish I could believe that!'

He circled her with his arms. 'Doesn't the fact that I'm here reassure you? I haven't mentioned a word of your latest suspicions and, if you haven't, there's no way Dr

Jenner can even suspect you are about to cause trouble for him.'

'Are you sure? You haven't made some enquiries, without telling me?'

He pulled her closer. 'I wish I could convince you to start trusting—'

'You have,' she broke in hurriedly, wanting to escape his hold. An amorous episode on their first evening was just what she didn't need. It would set a precedent that she already knew she would be unable to handle.

He raised a disbelieving eyebrow, but allowed her to free herself.

'I'm afraid I've eaten already, but I'll reheat some fish pie for you. Would that be OK?'

'I'm so hungry I could eat a shark, let alone a fish pie. I'd love it, please.'

As Fran moved through to the kitchen and switched on the oven she called over her shoulder, 'Would you like a drink while you wait? I've wine or beer.'

He acknowledged the choice. 'A glass of red wine would be very welcome.'

She nodded, and handed him a bottle from off the work surface. 'The corkscrew and glasses are behind you.'

When he'd removed the cork he placed the bottle beside the glasses. 'I'll leave it a moment to breathe.'

She nodded. 'The food won't be long.'

'I feel bad, causing you this extra work. It wasn't my fault, though. We had an emergency at the hospital.' His searching gaze sought forgiveness in her eyes.

'Who, or what, was that?'

'A new admission. A hip replacement discharged from the orthopaedic ward yesterday. She was readmitted with a pulmonary embolism.'

'Poor woman. If she only went home yesterday, she was very unlucky. I suppose she didn't move once she was home, allowing a blood clot to develop so quickly in her leg veins?'

Cal sighed. 'I think the damage was done before her discharge, but because she wanted to get home to her husband she didn't say anything about the pain in her calf. Rather than not moving, she probably did too much and caused a piece of the clot to break off and float up to her lungs.'

'Nasty.'

'It sure was. She was in deep shock and we nearly lost her a couple of times. She's hanging on in there at the moment, but it was touch and go.'

'Who's with her now?'

'Rob and the new reg, John. They should be able to cope.'

Fran slid some prepared vegetables into the microwave, then set the table with a cloth, knife and fork. Cal placed two filled wine glasses on the table and pulled up a couple of chairs.

Fran served out his food and placed the plate in front of him.

'Mmm. Smells delicious.' He sampled a forkful. 'Tastes it, too. Thanks, Fran. Perhaps I can reciprocate tomorrow?'

She raised her glass and toasted his offer. 'You don't know how good that sounds. By the time I've settled Naomi I often can't be bothered to prepare a proper meal for myself.'

He nodded. 'That's why you fainted at the antiques do.'

'I don't starve myself.' She defended herself hotly. 'I just find something that's easy.'

'Probably not enough after a hard day. I'll have to see what I can find to tempt you. Won't I?' he added, a lazy grin tugging at the corners of his mouth.

Sensing another meaning in his words, Fran tried to meet his searching gaze with equanimity, but failed miserably as he gave a wicked chuckle.

She tore her gaze away and fiddled with the stem of her wine glass.

'Hey, Fran. Lighten up. I'm aware of the house rules.'

When she didn't respond immediately he caught one of her hands in his. 'I know only too well that the last thing you need at the moment is further complications in your life, but that shouldn't stop us enjoying each other's company while this situation lasts.'

Relieved that he understood her fears, Fran allowed the breath to leave her body in a great rush. 'I'm sorry, Cal. I guess I find it so hard to believe anything good will ever come my way again that I'm always on the defensive.'

'Fran, you have as much right to happiness as the next person. Don't ever forget that. This nightmare will soon be over and you can start to build a normal life for your daughter. And for yourself.'

'I wish, but I won't hold my breath.'

'If you expect trouble that's what you'll get. You need faith.'

Fran dismissed his optimism with a laugh. 'I'll remember that when the next disaster strikes. Now, can I get you anything else to eat?'

'I'd love a coffee, but I'll make it myself. Lucky I know where everything is. And tomorrow I'll restock your larder.'

'I don't expect that. I've hired you as an unpaid bodyguard so the least I can do is feed you.'

Ignoring her protest, he switched on the kettle. 'Coffee for you?'

'Please.'

He found two mugs at the second attempt and, leaning lazily against the work surface, asked, 'Where would you like me to sleep? On the settee?'

As he spoke, Fran allowed her gaze to slide the length of his body and laughed. 'I think you might just hang over both edges. I've moved Naomi in with me and made up the spare bed.'

He nodded gratefully as he handed her the coffee.

'I'll try not to disturb you when I leave in the morning.'

Cal grinned. 'I'll probably be up before you. I like to take an early morning run.'

When they'd finished their coffee Fran showed him to his room. 'That's the bathroom. Naomi and I are next door.' She wanted him to be in no doubt.

'I'll pop down and do the dishes if you want to use the bathroom first.' He was about to speak when she continued, 'You don't have to go to bed yet but, as I'm on an early tomorrow, I will. You're welcome to the television.'

'Not tonight, thanks. I've brought a book. I need a good night's sleep myself.'

When she came back up the stairs he was just coming out of the bathroom. 'Goodnight, Fran. God bless.' He bent and she felt his lips graze the skin on her cheek.

The fragrance of his soap and toothpaste, mingled with his individual masculinity, invaded her nostrils. As she lay awake, savouring the lingering scent of him, she wondered if she was going to cope with them living in such close proximity. She found him far too attractive.

Naomi woke soon after six. Relieved that at least she'd slept through the night, without disturbing Cal, Fran lifted her from her cot and carried her down to the kitchen.

She was surprised to find Cal there before her, the electric kettle already singing its nearness to boiling point.

He turned and smiled at her. 'I heard Naomi and was going to bring you an early morning cup of tea.'

Feeling underdressed in her tartan shortie nightie, Fran murmured, 'That was kind of you, but I don't think Naomi is prepared to wait much longer for her breakfast.' Slinging the little girl expertly over one shoulder, she started to prepare a bowl of cereal with one hand.

Having poured water into the teapot, Cal left it to infuse and lifted Naomi from her.

'Come to Uncle Cal,' he murmured soothingly, as her small face puckered with indecision as to whether or not to cry. Sitting down, he danced her up and down gently on his knee, which made Naomi decide that a smile was the best option.

'If you're happy for a moment, I'll put something more on, then put Naomi in her chair and feed her.'

'Fine. We're getting on well here.'

Fran raced upstairs and slipped on a matching tartan dressing-gown. Feeling less vulnerable, she returned to the kitchen. As she did so, to her horror, she heard Naomi say, 'Dada. Dada.'

Colour flooded into Fran's cheeks as Cal turned to grin proudly at her. 'Did you hear that? She called me Dada!'

Unable to hide a suspicion that he'd been teaching her the word in her absence, she muttered, 'You know perfectly well that's the usual stringing together of sounds at this age—nothing more.'

She took Naomi from him and fastened her into her chair. Spooning cereal into her daughter's mouth, she told him tartly, 'If you're not going out for your run you can use the bathroom now. I'll be a little while here.'

He shrugged, placed a mug of tea within her reach and left the room, taking his own tea with him.

Fran closed her eyes for a moment and sighed deeply. 'What am I going to do, Naomi? He's everything I could ever want. Attractive, kind, thoughtful. Even you have turned traitor this morning to encourage him. And yet I know so little about him and, with my record, I really don't think I ought to get involved—however much I want to. Although I'm sure your dad would approve as well. Cal's so like him.'

Naomi gurgled happily in response, the cereal dribbling down her chin.

'I suppose it's my fault for agreeing to him moving in. But it seemed like a good idea at the time. I couldn't bear it if anything happened to you.'

Naomi responded happily, 'Dada. Dada.'

'I'll "Dada" you,' Fran said with a laugh. 'How about Mama for a change?'

But Naomi wasn't to be diverted. She'd found a new sound and wanted to keep trying it out. 'Dada...Dada.'

Fran checked her watch. 'Come on, drink up. We're getting late.' Naomi drank her milk greedily. 'By this time Cal should have surely finished in the bathroom.'

When he came down the stairs again Fran said, 'Help yourself to breakfast. Cereal in that cupboard, milk, eggs and bacon in the fridge.'

Cal nodded his thanks, then asked, 'Would you let me take Naomi to Jenny for you? That would give you more time.'

Fran became suddenly fiercely possessive. 'I think it's better if I do it. I don't want her upset for Jenny.'

Cal inclined his head. 'Why should she be? You saw her just now.'

Fran stammered, 'I—I know, b-but I was there with you then.'

'She didn't seem upset by our trip to the park either. It's up to you. If you'd like help with Naomi, I'm your man.'

Fran was torn. She didn't want to agree to his request, but neither did she want to antagonise him when he was being so kind. 'I think I'll have enough time.'

He nodded. 'I thought you might.'

Fran locked the bathroom door behind her, her heart racing. He was only doing what a bodyguard should do so why was she allowing his every word and action to have such a devastating effect on her? She should never have agreed to the arrangement, without knowing more about him first.

When she eventually made her way downstairs, carrying Naomi, he rose to greet her. 'Coffee?'

'I haven't time now, but I don't expect you to keep waiting on me any more than you expect me to wait on you.'

'Making coffee won't hurt me.'

'Before I go, this is the spare front door key to the cottage.'

'Thanks. I don't have to be at the unit until later so I'll try and make a few enquiries from Mrs Dubarry's neighbours.'

'You *will* be careful, won't you?'

'What do you think?'

Colour flooded into Fran's cheeks. 'You will.'

He nodded.

As she handed Naomi over she told Jenny that there had been threats, which was why she had intended to take a few days off work. 'However, Cal has moved in for the time being so I've decided to keep on at work.'

Her friend's eyes shone. 'Great. I knew he fancied you.'

'That's not the reason he's doing it. He thinks I ought to have a bodyguard. We've actually set firm boundaries to prevent either of us overstepping the mark.'

Jenny looked sceptical. 'I bet you don't keep to them.'

Fran was in too much of a hurry to argue. 'I must dash, but Cal wants me to warn you that he's trying to make a few enquiries about the doctor who threatened me this morning.'

'I'll keep the doors locked, I promise.'

Fran smiled. 'There shouldn't be any need, but just in case.'

When Fran arrived in the unit it was pandemonium.

When she could find one of the night shift nurses to ask why, she was told, 'Mrs Lucas, who was admitted yesterday evening, decided she was going home again. She was still attached to monitors and a drip and has made rather a mess of an expensive machine, as well as causing herself a relapse.'

'Who's with her?'

'Rob at the moment. He tried to contact Cal but he didn't answer his bleeper. He's asked us to try his mobile number as he knows Cal often goes out for a run early mornings, but it doesn't seem to be working today.'

Fran didn't want to admit that Cal was eating breakfast at her cottage at this very moment. He must have switched off his mobile so it didn't disturb Naomi and had forgotten to switch it on again.

'I'll...er...I'll give it another try.' She raced to the empty office and, closing the door, rang her home number.

Cal gave her number correctly. 'Cal, Rob needs your help with Mrs Lucas—he couldn't reach you on your mobile.'

He didn't ask for more information, just swore and said, 'I'll be right over.'

When Fran had relayed this information the senior night nurse took a moment to give her a quick report on the remainder of the patients, before escaping to her bed. Fran joined Rob behind the bed curtains and sent the remainder of the night staff off duty.

Rob was detailing what was needed when Cal joined them.

'What happened?'

Rob started his explanation again. 'The crash team appear to have her stabilised for the moment, but where do we go from here? We don't even know what dose of the anti-coagulants she'd received before she removed the infusion.'

As the crash team packed up their trolley Cal checked the relevant charts and then, after examining the patient briefly, indicated to Rob that they should move away and talk.

'Have you repeated the INR test?'

'The blood's just gone to the lab.'

'Set up the IV infusion again, and when we get the result we can decide what she needs in the way of anti-coagulants. She's started an oral dose, I presume?'

Rob nodded.

'Did she do any damage to her hip?'

'Apparently not.'

'There's not much else we can do at the moment, then, except work towards getting her home as soon as possible. She clearly doesn't like it here.'

It was past lunchtime before they had a moment for a break. 'That was a hairy morning, wasn't it?' Fran murmured as she handed Cal a mug of coffee.

'Mmm. Ruined any chance of starting my enquiries.'

Fran sighed deeply. 'It's not going to work, is it? It's almost as if... Oh! I'm being silly now.'

'No, you're not. Tell me, what is it "almost as if"?'

'Well, as if Dr Jenner somehow knows we're suspicious and is able to invisibly orchestrate events...just to prevent us knowing what he's up to.'

'You're being ridiculous now.' He leant across the desk and took her hands between his palms. 'I know how you must feel, Fran, but what happened this morning was merely coincidence.'

'How can you be sure?' Fran knew her voice was betraying her panic, but she could do nothing to control it. 'She's about the same age, from the same area of town—probably registered with the same doctor—'

Before she could finish, Cal interrupted calmly, 'You're overwrought. Mrs Lucas has a husband—that's the difference.' He waited for his words to sink through her rising hysteria. 'Come on, now, Fran. If we're to prove our suspicions we need to keep things in perspective.'

Suddenly ashamed of her outburst, Fran looked down at their entwined hands, resting on the desk. 'I'm sorry,' she mumbled. 'I can't stop worrying about Naomi. I really think it would be best if I give up work and keep her with me constantly.'

'No,' he told her firmly. 'You'd be a nervous wreck by the end of the first day. You need to get right away from the problem and delegate her care to those not quite so close to her. I know you trust Jenny and I hope you feel you can trust me.'

She nodded and released her hands. 'I do.'

He smiled. 'That's one step forward, then.'

'I suppose so,' she murmured dully, replacing her coffee-mug on the tray. 'However, I must find out what's happening on the ward in my absence.'

'And I want to take another look at Mrs Lucas.'

There wasn't a moment for them to chat again before the afternoon shift arrived so as she left she popped her head round Mrs Lucas's bed curtains and said to Cal, 'See you later.'

He nodded, and whispered, 'Don't forget, I'm cooking tonight. Your evening off.'

She smiled her acknowledgement and left, looking forward to the free time she now had available for her daughter. But when she arrived at Jenny's house the double-locked door made her fears return as strongly as ever.

Jenny took one look at her face and invited her in for a cuppa. 'Didn't you sleep?'

'It's not an easy time, is it?'

'Naomi's fine. Haven't heard a peep out of anyone.'

'Not surprising. Cal was called into work and so couldn't initiate any enquiries.'

When they'd finished their tea Jenny suggested, 'Let's wander down to the park. It'll do us both good.'

They were on their way home again when Fran said, 'I'll never, ever, be able to thank you enough, Jenny.'

'There's nothing to thank me for. You've already saved my sanity by letting me have a share in caring for your daughter. I'll never forget our meeting in the antenatal clinic—you wondering how you were going to manage alone with a child and me sure I'd never survive without! It's a wonder we didn't flood the place out with our tears that day!'

Fran laid a consoling hand on Jenny's arm. 'I got the best of the bargain.'

'No, you didn't. Having Naomi to care for helps me to relax and that should help me to conceive again.'

'I thought your doctor was going to refer you to a specialist.'

'He has, and we're assured there's no medical reason for my repeated miscarriages. So we're going for it one last time.'

They'd reached the house by this time, and as Jenny let herself in Fran followed her into the hall and gave her an enormous hug.

'I'll keep everything crossed that by this time next year you'll be caring for your own son or daughter.'

'And I'll keep everything crossed that you won't have to care for Naomi alone for much longer. Which reminds me, you'd better get home. Your "lodger" will wonder where you are, especially as it's getting dark already.'

'You don't believe that's all he is, do you? I know what you're insinuating and you're quite wrong.'

'Am I?' queried Jenny innocently. 'We'll see.'

When Fran arrived home Cal was preparing a ham and cream pasta bake.

'Mmm. That smells delicious. And do I detect newly baked bread?'

Cal nodded proudly. 'We can eat the moment Naomi's settled.'

The food was as good as it had promised to be, and Fran heaped praise on Cal's culinary expertise.

'I have to confess I didn't make the bread from scratch— it was part baked from the supermarket.'

'Whatever, it was a lovely treat.'

They lingered over coffee and chatted about the patients and their colleagues, but the subject of themselves seemed to be off limit. Every time Fran tried to learn a little more about him he neatly changed the subject.

Although she didn't have to be up early, Fran felt embarrassed at remaining downstairs with him. Although, or perhaps because, her emotions were acutely aroused by his proximity, she sought an excuse to escape, feigning tiredness with an enormous false yawn. 'I'll clear away, then I think I'm for bed.'

'My turn to see to the dishes tonight,' Cal told her. 'Have a good night.'

'I'm so tired I'm sure I will.' But she didn't. Instead, she heard his every move.

Naomi woke early next morning and Fran crept downstairs with her daughter in her arms, trying not to disturb Callum. He needed to make up for being disturbed the previous morning. She had heard him come up to bed not long after her, but she had made no sound that might have alerted him to the fact that she had still been awake. She was already convinced that him moving in had been a mistake. Although she hadn't expected to feel for another man the way she had about Daniel, she knew now that Cal had the power to unlock her feelings and she was afraid of making a fool of herself.

As she prepared her daughter's breakfast she tried to order her thoughts in a one-sided conversation. 'I'm afraid, Naomi. Afraid that I might hurt him deeply, afraid that I might hurt myself.'

'Dada,' Naomi agreed, as Fran slid her into her chair and started to feed her.

'You hungry too, Naomi?' Cal's jovial boom broke in on Fran's reverie and she realised that poor Naomi was waiting patiently, her mouth wide open, for the next spoonful of her breakfast cereal.

Hurriedly lifting the spoon to her daughter's mouth, Fran

murmured, 'Help yourself. There's cereal, toast, even eggs and bacon.'

He nodded. 'I'll just have a coffee, thanks.'

'I'm s-sorry if we disturbed you,' Fran stuttered, unnerved by him, standing over them.

'You didn't. I hope I didn't disturb *you* last night when I came to bed.'

'No. I didn't hear a thing.' She rushed to reassure him.

'You must have slept well, then.'

'I did,' Fran lied trough her teeth, not wanting him to know the effect he was having on her.

'You're on the late shift today, are you?'

Fran nodded.

'Any plans?'

'I'll take Naomi for a stroll and collect a few things from the shops, then leave her with Jenny after lunch.'

'Would you like me to collect her?'

His offer startled Fran. 'No, of course not. She's better off, staying with Jenny.' The mock-injured look on his face made her rush in with an explanation. 'She doesn't really know you well enough yet.'

He raised a quizzical eyebrow. 'You mean you don't?'

Her cheeks flaming, Fran protested, 'That's not fair. I don't want to be a burden to you. I'm more than grateful for what you're doing already, but I don't expect you to act as nursemaid as well.'

He smiled ruefully, but didn't argue. 'In that case, I'll use the time to follow up the enquiries I've made so far.'

'Is there anything I can do to help this morning?'

'No way.' This time his voice brooked no argument. 'The last thing we need is for Dr Jenner to hear *you're* poking around for information.' He poured himself a mug of coffee and refilled hers.

She tried to smile her thanks, but fear for her daughter, mixed with tiredness and the many other emotions she was experiencing, made her blink back tears at the same time.

'Lighten up, Fran.' Cal pulled up a chair beside her and, straddling it the wrong way, slipped a comforting arm around her shoulder. 'Try to remember you're not alone in this any more, and let other people help with your problems occasionally.'

She nodded. 'I guess I find that difficult because I've become too used to making all the decisions this past year.'

'I'm aware of that, Fran, but I intend to prove to you that sharing is much more fun. However, I promise I won't put pressure on you until you're ready.'

He leant forward and lightly kissed her cheek. 'I'll shower now and get out of your hair, if that's OK.'

'Fine.' She finished feeding Naomi in a daze as she tried to fathom the meaning of what he'd just said. Was he, after all, hinting at a relationship or was he merely suggesting that he wanted them to be friends? She wished she knew. It would make the coming days so much easier.

CHAPTER EIGHT

FRAN was still nursing a now wriggling Naomi when Cal ran down the stairs, exuding a scent of freshly washed masculinity.

'See you later in the unit, then?'

She nodded.

'Just be careful, and be sure to take your personal alarm with you everywhere.'

Fran nodded. 'I will. I promise. And don't you take any risks either.'

Clearly pleased at her concern for his safety, he grinned. 'I promise, ma'am. If I discover anything in the least incriminating I'll hand it straight over to the police.'

He closed the door behind him and she watched him stride jauntily to his car.

'Right, Naomi. Now we've got the house to ourselves it's bath first, then we'll feed the ducks.'

Fran enjoyed their morning together so much that she didn't realise how late it was getting. Consequently, she was later leaving for work than she'd intended.

She thanked Jenny briefly when she handed Naomi over, reminding her friend of the need for vigilance as Callum was trying again to make a few enquiries.

'No problem,' she said with a smile. 'Brian has secured this place like Fort Knox.'

Fran arrived at the unit just in time for the hand-over, but she had to force herself to concentrate on what was being said when she saw Callum, pacing impatiently up and down the corridor. The moment her colleagues from the morning shift had left the ward he burst into the office and closed the door behind him.

'Have you a moment, Fran?'

Relieved that she could trust Allie to alert her if any of her patients needed her immediate attention, she nodded. 'Have you made a momentous discovery?'

'I rather think I have. I spent my lunch hour gossiping.'

Fran was surprised. 'Who with?'

'Mrs Dubarry's neighbours. They don't miss a thing that's going on in their little patch.'

'So what had they to say about Dr Jenner?'

'There was general agreement that he couldn't have been more charming when they'd needed to consult him, but they were more than a mite suspicious when they saw him visit Mrs Dubarry's house soon after her death.'

'He visited her home? You mean...?'

'I'm not sure of anything yet, but he did have a key. I've checked with a couple of local estate agents, but neither have the house on their books. That's as far as I've got, but there must be something fishy. Even if she'd given him a key for when he visited, no doctor should need to go to the empty house after her death.'

'You've told the police?'

'I didn't have time, but after lunch I had a chat with the senior personnel officer. They're doing some delving at the moment.'

'So it's out of your hands?' Fran felt an unexpected surge of relief that he was no longer in danger.

'Possibly, but I'm not sure I want it to be. I quite enjoyed the challenge.'

'I would have thought you'd got enough challenges here—and, that being so, I must visit the patients and see what's needed.'

'I'll come with you, if that's OK. I haven't done a proper round today.'

While Fran prepared the notes trolley he opened the door, then turned back and said to her, 'You know what they say. A change is as good as a rest—and pretending to be a detective was certainly that!'

Pushing the trolley into the corridor, she said teasingly, 'And what about being a bodyguard? Is that restful too?'

'Depends who I'm guarding. Wouldn't you say?'

Realising she had played herself into an impossible position, she didn't answer but stalked ahead of him to where the first patient was sitting in a chair.

'Hello, Mrs Lucas,' Fran greeted her. 'You look much better than when I left you yesterday.'

She looked at each of them in turn. 'Can I go home, then?'

'Not yet.'

'But I thought you were short of beds.'

'That's as maybe,' Callum told her, 'but we don't throw patients out of beds they need.' He checked the charts at the foot of her bed and motioned Fran to draw the curtain round her for privacy before he listened to her chest.

'Much, much, better,' he told her eventually, 'but don't overdo it. And you're certainly not ready to leave us yet.'

As they moved on down the ward he murmured quietly to Fran, 'This generation hasn't much faith in us, has it?'

She shrugged. 'It's the newspapers. And television. The stories they put out must terrify someone of that age.'

As they reached Mrs Jenkins's empty bed he raised his eyebrow in silent acknowledgement of her statement. 'Any news of sheltered housing?'

'Mrs Jenkins is seeing the social worker now. I don't know if it's good news or bad.'

'Let's hope it's good. I don't think I can justify keeping her bed occupied for much longer.'

As they completed the round a smiling Mrs Jenkins came towards them. 'You'll never guess what's happened.'

'No,' Fran agreed.

'She's found me a small bungalow to rent where there's a warden if I need anything.'

'That's great news,' Cal enthused, winking at Fran over the patient's head. 'When can you move in?'

'The week after next. I'll be home before then, won't I? So I can pack up.'

'I can't see we need to keep you here much longer. What about us letting you home tomorrow?'

Mrs Jenkins was ecstatic. 'That should give me enough time. I'm sure my son will come down to help me. Thank you, Doctor. And you too, Nurse.'

'We'll arrange it, then.'

As they walked back up the ward Cal murmured, 'See. Contrary to your expectations, things do work out sometimes.'

'It might not be Mrs Chambers's bungalow she's moving into.'

He laughed. 'You don't give up, do you? It doesn't matter whether it's hers or not, Fran. You alerting the social worker that her need was urgent did the trick, I'm sure.'

'Maybe.'

Cal sighed and shook his head. 'There's no maybe about it. If I wasn't desperate for a coffee I'd drag you along to the social work office and prove it. As I am, you'll have to take my word for it.'

He pushed the notes trolley into the office for her and closed the door behind them. 'And, as you're working late, I'll make you a celebratory meal tonight.'

'What on earth for?'

'For Mrs Jenkins's new home, of course.'

'Oh! I see.' For a moment she'd been afraid—or possibly hoped—that he'd had a more personal reason.

'If there's nothing more you want me for, I must go and help Allie, otherwise it'll be time for the drug round.'

He nodded. 'I'll get out of your way, then. See you later. You're sure you don't want me to pick Naomi up?'

'I think it's best for her to remain with someone she knows well, thanks.' Fran was aware it would save her a trip after work, but she wasn't prepared to sanction any change in Naomi's routine that might upset her—at least, not for the time being. It was especially pointless when Cal might soon be gone. Once Dr Jenner realised the game was up there would be no reason for Cal to remain at the cottage.

It was later than usual when Fran arrived home with Naomi, but just knowing someone was there was fantastic. When she opened the front door the delicious smell which filled the cottage was a bonus.

He came out of the kitchen. 'Do you want anything for Naomi?'

'She's dead to the world. I'll put her straight into her cot.' She carried her small charge upstairs and Cal shut the door behind her.

When she came downstairs again she felt almost shy at the sight of the beautifully decorated table with candles.

'I thought we'd celebrate in style,' he said. 'Would madam like a pre-dinner drink?'

Fran shook her head. 'Not when I'm on an early morning.'

He nodded. 'Then the choice of starter is melon or melon with prawns.'

'Melon with prawns sounds delicious.'

Cal bantered his way through the remainder of the meal, and Fran gradually relaxed. 'It's all superb,' she told him as a raspberry *crème brûlée* followed the main course of duck. 'I didn't know you were such an expert cook.'

He grinned. 'I'm not, but I know an extremely good convenience counter.'

'They've done you proud.' She felt so contented that she went on to tease him. 'You'll have to introduce me to it, then I won't faint at your feet again.'

'In that case, I'll keep the secret close to my chest,' he told her with an infectious grin that did incredible things to his eyes—and her blood pressure. 'Now, would madam like to come into the lounge for her coffee?'

'Thank you.' Fran moved to the nearest armchair and, after refilling their glasses with the red wine which had accompanied the meal, he placed her glass within easy reach.

'This is luxury,' she joked. 'I could adapt to this way of life quite easily.'

He seated himself where he could look into her face and said seriously, 'It's only what you deserve.'

Wary of what he might be leading up to, her eyes met and held his. 'I'd probably soon tire of it!' she told him, her lips twitching with amusement.

He shook his head ruefully, releasing their eye contact. 'I don't think so somehow.' He took both her hands in his and she wanted him to kiss her, but although his eyes were soft he made no move towards her.

'You are so lovely, Fran. Why did we agree to such rigid boundaries?'

Can I handle this? she thought, as panic merged with excitement to make her heart quicken uncomfortably. She lowered her eyes to hide an unbidden tear and murmured mistily, 'I think it's a good thing we did.'

He lifted her chin with his forefinger and smiled at her. 'If you mean, as I believe you do, that you'd be tempted, too, perhaps—perhaps we should relax the parameters a little.'

'No,' she spluttered, scared by her own response to him. 'That's the last thing we should do.'

He moved closer and took her in his arms. 'Why, Fran? We're both free agents and—'

'Are you?' She pulled away from him, her eyes blazing with accusation. 'I don't know that. I know nothing at all about you.'

He released her, muttering, 'How much do you need to

know before you trust me?' He strode into the kitchen and poured out the coffee he had offered earlier.

When he returned to sit opposite her she said quietly, 'You wouldn't be here with me now if I didn't trust you, Cal, but I'd still like to know a little more about you. After all, you've winkled out *my* life history.'

'I trained as a doctor in Glasgow and, like all medics, have moved on pretty regularly, gradually southwards. I worked with Mrs Wood in Essex, as I've already told you.'

'But where do you live now? I had no idea where to contact you when you were so late moving in here.'

'I have a small house by the river on the boundary between Wenton and Riverlands.'

'Do you live there alone?'

'Most of the time.'

Aware that he was probably teasing her, she guessed he thought she'd gone too far already with her inquisition, but if she was to allow him any closer she needed to know.

Cal must have sensed her inward struggle and he held out his left hand towards her. 'See. Nothing on the ring finger and no mark where I've removed a ring.' The glitter in his eyes told her he was no longer joking. 'Satisfied?'

Although well aware that many married doctors didn't wear wedding rings, she realised it would be prudent to pretend to accept his word, at least while he remained her resident bodyguard.

'It might be useful, though, if you don't object, if I have the telephone number of your home. Just in case of an emergency.' The moment she'd finished speaking, she saw it had been a suggestion too far.

'So you can check up on me?' he snapped. 'My mobile and my bleeper are sufficient for most people.' He scribbled a number on a page of his Filofax and, tearing it roughly, threw it onto the coffee-table.

Fran drained her coffee-cup and stood up. 'I'm sorry if I've upset you, Cal. I didn't intend to, but it is nice to know a bit more about the man I've invited into my home.' She spoke quietly but firmly. 'Thank you for the lovely meal. I'll clear the dishes and then I'm off to bed. Early shift tomorrow.'

He sprang to his feet and took her arm. 'I'm sorry. I overreacted. Celtic blood and all that! I'll do the dishes tonight. You get off to bed. No hard feelings?' He leaned closer and dropped a light kiss onto her cheek.

'None at all. And you were right. I *was* tempted earlier to change the rules, but I think as long as we are in this abnormal situation it wouldn't be wise. For either of us.'

He sighed deeply. 'You're probably right. Goodnight, Fran, and God bless.'

She made her way quietly up to her room, undressed in the dark and slid beneath the duvet, without waking Naomi. But it took a long time for sleep to claim her. She could hear Cal moving about downstairs and she tried to visualise what it would be like, making love with him. Because, if she was honest with herself, that was what she'd wanted to do since the day they'd first met.

She was right not to, though. Wasn't she? Thrown together like this, they could make a big mistake, and when the time came for him to move out she would be the one left hurting. As she had been with Daniel.

She had showered and washed and fed Naomi before Cal appeared in the kitchen the next morning. 'I'm just leaving. There's coffee in the pot.'

He nodded, and ran his hands through his tousled hair. 'Sorry, I didn't hear you about.'

'No problem,' she reassured him. 'I'll leave you to lock up. OK?'

'See you later, then.'

'I'll look forward to that.'

His blue eyes crinkled at her response, ruining her efforts to ignore his well-proportioned torso, naked from the waist up. Fran felt her heart quicken treacherously.

'I'll get us a meal tonight,' she offered, to hide her confusion.

'I wondered if Jenny would look after Naomi and let us go out to eat this evening.'

'I'll ask her, but as it's Friday she probably has plans already.'

'Tomorrow or Sunday, then?'

Fran nodded. 'I'll ask. I must go now or I'll be late.'

Questions niggled at her mind throughout the drive to work. Had he invited her out because he enjoyed her company or was he hoping it might persuade her to bend the rules? She supposed it might even be because he was tired of washing their dishes!

Jenny *was* available to babysit, and as she carried out her early morning tasks Fran decided that Cal was trying to prove that his interest in her wasn't just because they'd been thrown together.

She was doing the morning drug round when she saw him, coming in search of her. 'Hi. Any problems?'

Fran shook her head as she locked up the drug trolley, then, as he ushered her into the office, she said, 'Only Mrs Jenkins. She needs a letter for her doctor and you said you'd like to do it yourself.'

'Will she be in the same doctor's area when she moves to the sheltered accommodation?'

'Apparently.'

'I'll give her a brief note for him, but I think I'll also ring him and have a chat about her. What time's she going?'

'Could be anytime. Hopefully, this morning, but with hospital transport you never know.'

'I've accepted a patient for her bed this afternoon.'

'No problem. Mrs J. can wait in the day room. What's the problem with the new admission?'

'Another anaemia, and her GP doesn't know why. She's for blood transfusion and investigations.'

'Not eating properly?'

'Dr Purdy thinks it's more than that.'

'Dr Purdy?' Fran queried. 'We seem to be getting a lot of his patients at the moment.'

'I don't think there's anything suspicious about this one, but when he rang it gave me a chance to ask about you know who. He's already moved on to another job, but Dr Purdy knows he's done the odd shift here on his days off and thinks we want to employ him again so he's sending me his CV and details of where to contact him.'

Fran closed the office door cautiously. 'Have you found out anything more about him?'

Cal shook his head. 'Nothing concrete, but the moment the fax of his CV arrives I'll hand it to Personnel who contacted the police this morning.'

'This morning? Why didn't you tell me earlier? I could have warned Jenny. I must ring her now.'

Cal put his hand over the receiver as she tried to lift it. 'Calm down. I only found out half an hour ago myself and I rang Jenny immediately.'

Fran shivered uncontrollably. 'I—I'd rather be with Naomi myself. Do—do you think—?'

'Jenny is being ultra-careful. When you go and collect Naomi this afternoon I suggest you stay with Jenny until I finish here, then I'll escort you both back to the cottage. We've both got the weekend off and by Monday it should hopefully be all resolved.'

Her eyes wide with fear, Fran demanded, 'Do you really think so? I—I—'

Cal pulled her towards him in a comforting hug. 'It'll soon be all over, love. And I'll be there for you until it is. And afterwards—'

Overwrought, Fran clung to him, disregarding all her earlier resolve. She didn't wait to hear what he was about to say. 'I—I won't go out for a meal tonight, Cal. I'm not leaving Naomi.'

'That's fine. We'll eat out tomorrow lunchtime and take Naomi with us. OK?'

Fran nodded, but for the remainder of the morning she found it difficult to concentrate on her patients' needs. The moment she had given the hand-over report she left the hospital at speed.

Jenny didn't open the door immediately. She identified Fran first through the peephole viewer and even then left the chain on the door until she saw that Fran was alone.

'Come in. The kettle's on.'

Fran did so eagerly and Jenny locked the door behind them. 'Where's Naomi?'

'In here.' Jenny led the way into the back room and Fran had never been so pleased to see her daughter safe and well as she was at that moment. 'Cal said you are going to wait here until he finishes work.'

Fran nodded. 'If that's all right by you. And, Jenny, we won't be going out this evening after all. I couldn't bear to leave her for a moment.'

'I'm not surprised.'

They watched Naomi, playing happily, while they drank their tea, but their conversation was spasmodic. Fran couldn't keep her mind on anything, apart from wondering what action the police were taking and whether Cal had given them Dr Jenner's CV.

When the doorbell rang just after five Fran ran towards it with Jenny in hot pursuit, warning, 'Don't open it until you've checked who it is, Fran.'

Fran did as she was told and was relieved to see Cal on the doorstep. 'Cal, thank goodness.' Fran blinked back the tears which were threatening as she pulled the door ajar. 'Has anything happened?'

'Not that I'm aware of. Can I come in?'

Fran hurriedly took the door off the chain and opened it wide. 'Naomi's in here.'

While Fran led Cal to the back room Jenny relocked the door and switched on the kettle again. 'Coffee or tea, Cal?'

'Coffee would be great, please.'

For Jenny's sake they waited until Brian came home from work, then Fran and Cal left with Naomi. As they made their way to the car Fran looked round nervously and Naomi, sensing her tension, started to scream.

'I'm parked right behind you,' Cal told Fran, 'so take your time, securing Naomi in her seat, and I'll keep my eyes skinned.'

When she pulled into the drive of the cottage Fran realised she didn't remember anything of the drive home. Her nerves were raw with anxiety, not to mention apprehension about the coming weekend with Cal.

He pulled up behind her and, taking her keys, opened the door so that she could carry Naomi straight indoors. Cal locked the car and the front door behind them and went round the house to double-check that all the windows were secure.

'Now you can stop fretting and relax.'

'I'll give Naomi her tea and get her to bed. Then I'll forage for our supper.' Fran was agitated—anything to keep busy.

'Stop trying to be a supermum and let me do something to help.'

Fran looked up at him angrily. 'You can get us a meal later, then.'

His nod was resigned. 'OK. I'll do whatever I'm told. What do you fancy?'

'There's a frozen pizza. And plenty of salad. Or—'

'That would be fine. Or we could have a pizza delivered.'

'No.' Fran's reply was a shout of anguish. 'We don't want strangers at the door.'

'Fran,' he said, 'be reasonable. It would only be a delivery boy. How could Dr Jenner know about that?'

'He might be listening in to my telephone calls.'

'Now you are being ridiculous. Anyway, there's no problem. I can use my mobile.'

'No,' responded Fran sharply. 'That's stupid. They're even more accessible to eavesdroppers.'

'Not the type I have.' He sighed deeply. 'But don't fret. It's not important. Frozen pizza it shall be.'

Fran knew he was exasperated by her fears, but as she bathed Naomi she told her daughter that at least their disagreements would stop them getting too close!

Naomi must have sensed the angst between them because she took much longer to settle than usual. Consequently, it was nearly ten before they sat down to their meal, a light classical CD playing quietly in the background.

Cal had brought a bottle of red wine and Fran saw it was already opened and breathing as she seated herself at the table.

'Wine?' He lifted the bottle, but she covered the glass with her hand.

'Not tonight, Cal. I want to be alert.'

He replaced the bottle on the table. 'One glass of a wine you enjoy won't hurt, and it might help you to relax a little.'

Aware that he'd gone to the trouble of finding her favourite wine, Fran perversely felt her temper rise. 'I don't want to relax.'

He lifted his eyebrows and shook his head. 'We are contrary tonight, aren't we?'

'Stop patronising me.'

'I can't do anything right, can I? Is it only because of your fears for Naomi—or are you afraid of your own feelings?'

Fran gasped. 'It's been a long day and I'm tired. That's all.'

He shrugged. 'You don't mind if I drink, do you?'

They ate their pizza in silence and Cal consumed a couple of glasses of wine.

He didn't ask her again, and she regretted her earlier refusal, but was determined not to ask for any wine.

When the meal was over he cleared the plates and said, 'I'm making coffee. Do you want one before you go to bed?'

If she wouldn't have woken Naomi, Fran would have screamed. Now she was being sent to bed in her own home, and yet she knew it was only because she'd told him she was tired. She had to admit that it *was* her feelings for him, mixed with her fears for her daughter, that were making her behave so badly.

'I would like a coffee, thanks.'

He brought it through to her and they moved to the armchairs.

When she'd finished the coffee she thanked Cal for the food and told him to leave the dishes until the morning. 'I'm off to bed now. Goodnight, Cal.'

As she rose from her chair he crossed the room and pulled her to him. 'Sleep well, Fran. And don't worry. I *do* understand what you're going through.' As he spoke she felt his muscles hardening against her body and she moved quickly away.

She felt like a heel as she cleaned her teeth and climbed into bed, but if she wasn't to make a fool of herself with a man for the second time what else could she do?

Naomi woke early as usual next morning, and Fran crept downstairs with her before she could disturb Cal.

She'd finished feeding her and had had a leisurely breakfast herself by the time Cal put in an appearance.

She was apprehensive after her behaviour the previous evening, but he greeted her warmly and kissed Naomi on the cheek. 'Hi, trouble.'

Fran smiled tentatively. 'Coffee in the pot. What would you like for breakfast?'

'Coffee. As I promised yesterday, I'm taking you and Naomi out for lunch and I don't want to spoil my appetite.'

'Where?'

'Wait and see.'

They visited a nearby National Trust house, which had a superb restaurant attached where Naomi was welcome.

They had a great day together. Fran could sense the relationship between Cal and Naomi building, and she knew that, despite her reservations, she felt the same way.

When they arrived back at the cottage Cal unlocked the door and checked all was well, before allowing Fran in. She realised that she had enjoyed the day so much she'd almost forgotten why she needed a bodyguard.

She made a cup of tea while he chatted nonsensically to Naomi. When they'd finished she said, 'Naomi's tired. She didn't settle very early last night so I'm going to get her to bed soon.'

'I'd like to feed her and bath her,' he told her quietly. 'Give you a break for once.'

Fran was about to say no, then capitulated. 'OK. If you really want to.'

He grinned. 'I do, and I'm a dab hand at bathing, I promise.'

While he took care of Naomi Fran searched out the ingredients for an Indonesian fried rice dish, nasi goreng, then settled back to watch how he coped.

His expertise reawakened her suspicions. He hadn't actually denied ever being married or even having children of his own. He'd skilfully skirted the question by showing her his empty ring finger. There was so much she still didn't know about him and yet she was hopelessly in love with him.

The happy sounds coming from the bathroom drew her like a magnet to see what was happening.

Both Naomi and Cal were having a wonderful time, splashing water everywhere. He turned and smiled at her, filling her heart with even more love for him. She returned his smile as he lifted her daughter from the bath and wrapped her in a fluffy towel.

Fran was about to hand him the tiny vest when the telephone downstairs rang imperiously.

'Back in a mo,' she told him, wanting to share his obvious enjoyment.

She lifted the receiver, giving her number, but the voice at the other end was already speaking. Then the line was cut. The receiver slid from Fran's shocked grasp and she sat heavily on the nearest chair, tears slithering down her cheeks. It was too much. They had all been so happy a minute earlier and now it had been destroyed.

She heard Cal, coming down the stairs. 'Do you want to put her into her cot?' he called, then, seeing her face, asked, 'What on earth's the matter?'

'It was…was Dr Jenner, I think. He didn't actually say— all he said was not to forget the danger for Naomi and not to go to the police. Then he uttered a chilling laugh and hung up.

'Oh, Cal, I'm frightened. He knows too much about us. He must know our every move, otherwise why would he have rung tonight?' Fran was sobbing as if her heart would break.

Without another word, Cal turned and carried Naomi upstairs. He must have placed her in her cot and set her musical toy playing because Fran could hear the familiar tinkle of Brahm's Lullaby.

He came back downstairs and lifted the receiver, then replaced it, before taking Fran into his arms. 'You're freezing, love. Come through and tell me all about it.' He led her to the settee and, sitting down beside her, wrapped his arms closely round her.

She shuddered violently and Cal pulled her even closer. Bending his head, he searched out her lips and kissed her. His kiss of comfort deepened and Fran succumbed. Again and again and again he kissed her, gradually stifling her sobbing with his kisses.

When she was still he lifted a hand to wipe away the tears, then murmured, 'There's no need for you to contact the police or for them to contact you so there will be no reason for him to do anything to Naomi.'

'He must know the police are involved though, mustn't he? How?'

'It seems so—he's obviously a smart operator.'

Tears were gathering in her eyes again and he gently lifted her onto his lap. 'We're safe here, love,' he murmured into her hair. 'There's no way he can reach Naomi as long as she's here with us both.'

'But how will we know what's happening? When or if it's safe to go out again? We both have to go to work on Monday. What then? We daren't ring the police. He may have the telephone tapped—or anything.' Her voice was rising hysterically and Cal hugged her tightly.

'Calm down. I told the personnel department I was living here for the time being, and they're sure to pass that on to the police. One or the other will contact us if there are any developments. And there's always my mobile.'

Her fears resurfaced and Fran pushed herself away from his chest so that she could look up into his face. 'No. He's too clever. He'll intercept the call somehow.'

He was about to protest when another worrying thought struck her. 'Cal. What will Personnel think about us, living together?'

'They're not guardians of our morals, Fran. But I did tell them why I was doing it.'

'I know, but—'

'But nothing, and if our characters are going to be ruined, we might as well make it worthwhile. There's plenty we can be doing here to fill the time. Like this.'

She looked up to see what he meant and his lips met hers as her head went back. The exquisite sensations he aroused toppled her into an overwhelming helplessness as he increased the pressure, probing with his tongue until she parted her lips and allowed the invasive moistness of his tongue to tangle with her own.

The unique scent and taste of him was almost more than Fran could bear, and she was cocooned in a floating sensation from which she didn't want to surface.

When eventually he lifted his lips away the magic ended, and Fran felt an acute sense of loss that allowed her fears to flood back, unchecked.

He laid his cheek against hers and must have felt the tears, again spilling down her cheeks. 'I know it's not easy, love, but it'll soon be over.'

She turned and clung to him. 'How can you know that?'

'It must be somebody or other's law.'

She knew his joke was meant to cheer her, but things were too black for her to appreciate it. 'Don't leave me until it is, Cal. Please.'

'Now why should I do that when I've appointed myself your bodyguard?'

She looked up at him, suddenly aghast. 'You're doing that for me and I haven't fed you.'

She started to move away and he pulled her back. 'We ate enough at lunchtime to keep us going all weekend.'

She shook her head and clung to him. 'But, Cal, I'm so frightened. If I cook us a meal, it might help me calm down.'

'We don't have to eat—there are other ways of doing that.'

'I don't want to be left alone. Say you'll stay down here with me,' she cried anxiously. 'All night?'

'I can do better than that,' he told her softly.

He lifted her gently and carried her upstairs to his room. 'Sorry about the single bed, but this way we won't wake Naomi,' he whispered.

'Cal...' Fran knew she should protest, but her mouth was

dry and her heart, thudding painfully against her ribs, made it impossible for her to get her breath.

He pulled back the duvet and slid her beneath it. The scent of him on the covers told her she had reached the point of no return and she knew, despite all her earlier reservations, that it was right.

After a quick visit to the bathroom he joined her. 'We'll leave the lights on downstairs and our bedroom doors open.'

She made room for him under the single duvet, and when he took her in his arms again she offered no resistance. He wanted her and she needed his comfort.

CHAPTER NINE

FRAN awoke to broad daylight, and for a moment couldn't place where she was.

Her cheeks flushed as she recalled her abandoned behaviour of the night before, and she turned to find out if Cal was awake.

There was no sign of him, and his clothes, which she now remembered him dropping into an untidy pile at the foot of the bed, were missing too.

She sprang out of bed, fear contracting her heart painfully. Naomi! Why hadn't she woken Fran at the usual early hour?

The cot was empty. Fran uttered a shriek of terror and—stopping only to retrieve her nightshirt—raced downstairs to find Naomi in her high chair, chuntering happily between spoonfuls of breakfast fed by Callum.

Fran stopped abruptly, staring at them as if they were aliens from outer space.

'What—? Why—? Why on earth didn't you waken me?' She yawned widely.

He smiled at her. 'You needed the sleep. We're fine here, but please don't repeat that banshee wail. We nearly spilt the cereal between us.'

'I—I thought Naomi— Well, I didn't know where she was and—and—'

'You thought she'd been kidnapped.'

Fran slumped into a dining chair and rested her elbows on the table to support her head. 'You shouldn't have taken her, without waking me. I—I didn't know what had happened to her. I was—' To her dismay Fran heard her voice crack and she was fighting back tears again.

Cal crossed the room in one stride and cradled her in his arms. 'It was purely to give you a lie-in. The last thing I intended was to frighten you.'

'I know.' Fran reached for a tissue and blew her nose noisily. 'I'm OK now.' She raised her eyes and gave him a watery smile. 'I'm not very grateful, am I? Several days this last week I'd have given anything for a lie-in.'

His lips found hers with a gentle certainty. 'I'd have given anything to stay there with you this morning,' he murmured. She felt him stir against her and Fran knew her body was sending its own messages to him.

'I'm not sure that would have been a good idea.'

'Why? I thought we were good together last night.'

'It's morning now.'

'Are you trying to tell me last night was wrong?'

Pursing her lips, she shook her head. 'But I don't think we should repeat it. I was upset then—'

'And you're not this morning? You just—'

The end of his sentence was drowned by Naomi, giving an indignant yell. Fran laughed. 'She's objecting to her breakfast being interrupted so rudely. Naomi insists on being put first, I'm afraid.'

She slid out of his hold and took over the feeding routine, but as she lifted the first spoonful she peeked back at Cal with a mischievous grin.

He pretended to be offended. 'As I'm obviously no longer necessary, I'll take a shower.'

'I didn't say that,' she responded archly. '*I* need you...'

'You do?' He swung round, and she caught a tenderness in his expression that left her in no doubt of his thoughts.

She deliberately misunderstood. 'Yes. As long as Dr Jenner is at large Naomi and I need a bodyguard, which leaves you no time for other activities.'

He gave her a penetratingly straight look. 'It had better be a cold shower, then.' He stomped up the stairs as Fran laughed wickedly.

When he came downstairs again, freshly showered, she grinned. 'My turn now. And Naomi's. She's not smelling too fresh at the moment.'

'I did change her nappy before I fed her,' he told her indignantly.

'Well, she didn't think much of having a clean one, then!'

When they came down again, both smelling much sweeter, he took Naomi from Fran's arms and kissed them both on the cheek.

'What would you like to do today?' he asked Fran, as he dandled Naomi on his knee.

'With Mum and Dad arriving on Wednesday, I had thought about housework, but you've done a pretty good job already.' She looked round the room appreciatively.

'It's all superficial.'

'Whatever, the place looks great.'

'So, where would you like to go?'

Fran was unsure what his reaction might be if she told him the truth, but she decided to risk it, especially as she remembered him saying that she ought to have faith.

Despite the events of the previous evening, there was still a lot they had to learn about one another.

'Before I returned to work I went to church on Sunday mornings. And I'd like to go today. They do have a crèche, which I sometimes use, but I wouldn't be happy to let Naomi out of my sight today. What about you?'

'Would you like to leave Naomi here with me?'

She shook her head, wondering if this was Cal's way of evading going to church. 'It's no problem. She can stay with us as long as she's quiet, and if not we can go to the back. That's if you'd like to go.'

'In that case, I'll come with you. Always supposing your church will allow in a Presbyterian!'

'They'll allow anybody!'

When he laughed Fran compressed her lips thoughtfully.

Was he coming as their bodyguard, or because she was going, or did he really want to go to a church service? Once more, she realised, she had made it easy for him to avoid giving a direct answer.

'We'll go out to Sunday lunch afterwards. While you get ready I'll book a table.'

He took them to lunch in a thirteenth-century manor house, which had been converted into a small hotel.

There were log fires blazing in the grates and the owner welcomed them in an attractive and homely lounge. After they'd eaten they returned there for coffee and lingered far into the afternoon.

'Feeling better?' Cal asked Fran, when they were thinking about leaving.

She nodded. 'Somehow going to church made things seem not so bad, and being here has made me realise that life is still going on around us, however uptight about things I might be.'

Over a shared tea, with Naomi scattering crumbs everywhere, Fran asked, 'What are we going to do about work tomorrow? I'm on a late and you'll be still at work when I'm due on duty.'

Cal was thoughtful. 'That is a problem. Until this matter is settled I don't want to leave you alone with Naomi. Neither do I think we should put Jenny in danger. Perhaps I'll give the police a call on the mobile and see what's happening.'

'You can't, Cal.' She panicked. 'He's far too clever. He'll find out somehow. Please, Cal, don't. Please!'

'We can't just sit here and wait. We're both expected at the hospital tomorrow.'

Fran sighed deeply and shuddered. 'Oh! Cal, I'm frightened. I felt so secure earlier. Now all my fears are crowding back in again.'

He took the seat beside her on the settee and cradled her

in his arms. 'Don't fret, love. There's a way around it. We can drive to the police station, taking Naomi with us, and explain about last night's threat. We'll ask for protection for you while I'm at work. I'll tell the hospital you have to take a couple of days off.'

She buried her head in his chest, trying to blink back her tears. 'It won't be the same as having you here.'

He lifted her head and, after kissing her softly, said to her, 'That's the nicest thing you've ever said to me.'

Despite her worries, she smiled up at him with wet eyes. 'I was only complimenting your work as a bodyguard...'

'Does that mean you'll invite the police into your bed the moment my back is turned?'

Her cheeks flared with colour as she recalled that the previous evening she had done something she had vowed would never happen again after Daniel. And she'd known even less about Cal than she had about Daniel!

He pressed the question she hadn't answered. 'Well, would you?'

Embarrassed, she said, 'I seem to have given you a completely wrong impression. I didn't intend last night to happen. I was just...just so churned up by that phone call that I didn't really know what I was doing.'

'Well, thank you very much,' he told her dryly.

Confused, Fran rushed on to explain, 'I didn't mean... Oh, I can't explain.' The tears which had been threatening for so long trickled down her cheeks.

'You have to admit you have the darndest way of putting things.'

'I'm sorry, Cal. I do appreciate all you've done for us both...'

'But?'

'There isn't any but.'

'No?'

When she didn't answer he suggested, 'Let's get Naomi ready for bed before we make our trip to the police station.'

Fran was subdued as they shared her bathtime. They were preparing to leave when the telephone rang. Fran jumped and clutched Naomi, turning to Cal with a terrified expression. 'I don't want to answer it. I couldn't bear to hear that man again.'

Cal removed the receiver and, placing it to his ear, said coolly, 'Yes?'

He listened in silence for what seemed like hours to Fran, and her panic must have been visible to Cal for he held out a placatory hand.

'That's great, then. Thank you for letting us know.' he told the voice at the other end.

As he replaced the receiver Fran demanded, 'Who was it? What?'

'It was the police. They've arrested Dr Jenner. He's in custody for trying to gain pecuniary advantage by deception. At least, I think that was what they said.'

'What does it mean?'

'Using a false CV! Apparently, he was bogus after all.'

'Can they keep him in prison for that?'

'I don't know all the details, but if he did it to allow him to treat patients when he wasn't qualified, and they can prove he has neglected those patients for financial gain, I should think they could lock the door and throw away the key.'

'Do you mean,' she gasped between the kisses he was raining on her, 'do you mean there's no threat any longer?'

'Not for the moment. They say he's unable to raise bail.'

'Oh! Cal.' Fran was torn between ecstatic relief and the sudden realisation that the need for a bodyguard had disappeared.

'My prayers this morning have been answered,' he told her. 'Come on. Let's celebrate. I'll rustle us up something to eat.'

He made an omelette similar to the one she had first cooked for him, and he also produced another bottle of the wine she had so discourteously rejected on Friday night. This time she didn't refuse!

As they ate and drank, Fran became increasingly morose as she realised he would move out now they no longer needed a bodyguard.

'What's the matter?' he asked, refilling her glass. 'I thought you'd be feeling as if you've won the lottery. Instead, you look as if you've lost the winning ticket.'

She sighed. 'I'm delighted with the news about Dr Jenner.'

'Another B-U-T?' he spelled out.

'I ought to let Jenny know I'll need her tomorrow.'

He frowned. 'That's no problem. You only need to pick up the phone.'

Fran nodded. 'I'll do it in a minute.'

'There's something else, isn't there?'

Fran felt unable to voice her fears. After all, he'd never said he loved her, never made any commitment to her. It would be better if he left that evening and yet she couldn't just throw him out. 'No, I don't think so. I was just wondering,' she lied airily, 'if you are going to return home tonight.'

His answering look was incredibly tender. 'Do you want me to?'

'You are welcome to stay as long as you like. I just thought you'd prefer it that way.'

'You don't fool me, Fran. You are looking at that half-empty glass again.'

'What?' Her glass was full of wine.

'I'm talking about that optimism I was going to infuse you with. I don't seem to have managed it. I expected you to be over the moon at the news, but instead you're looking ahead to the next problem.'

'I—'

'You worried me for a moment,' he continued. 'I thought

you wanted me out of the house as soon as possible now I've served my purpose, but it's not that, is it?'

She no longer knew what she did want, apart from not returning to a lonely existence. If he went, she and Naomi would revert to life as it had been before. Or could they? Would their life ever be the same?

'I—I shouldn't have behaved the way I did last night.'

'You shouldn't.'

She wasn't sure if his response was a query or a statement.

'I should have learnt my lesson the first time, instead of making the same mistake again.'

'I didn't think it was a mistake last night,' he told her quietly.

The smile that lurked around the corner of his mouth suggested he was teasing, but Fran wasn't sure enough of him to know.

'It's different for men. There's not the commitment.' Especially when there was another man's child involved, she finished silently.

'I'm sorry you don't think so.' He was clearly hurt by her words. 'As I've been drinking, I'd like to stay one more night as I need my car for work tomorrow. However, I promise not to compromise your space.'

She was suddenly contrite, wanting to explain that she was trying to give him the means to escape if he regretted what had taken place between them. 'I wasn't accusing you, Cal. It was— '

'Whatever,' he interrupted. 'I'll clear away the dishes while you use the bathroom. I'll try not to wake you when I leave for work.'

He was giving her the clearest indication possible that she was quite safe and the sooner he could leave the better. And it was all her fault for attempting to force the issue to her own satisfaction.

Wanting to feel his arms around her again, she tried to make amends. 'I'm sorry, Cal. Please try to understand—'

'I do. I do. Goodnight, Fran.' He carried the plates and glasses into the kitchen.

There was nothing to do but make her way up the stairs, but before she did so she rang and told Jenny the news. 'So we hope to be with you as usual after lunch.'

'Goodnight, Cal,' she called to his back view, resolutely hunched over the washing-up. 'I really *am* grateful for all you've done, you know.'

There was no response.

She was feeding Naomi in the kitchen the next morning when Cal came down from the bathroom ready for work, and her heart plummeted when she saw he was carrying his overnight bag.

'Coffee?' she offered.

'I'll get one later, thanks. See you in the unit some time.'

She felt bereft when he slammed the door behind him, but she knew it was her own fault. It was her lack of trust that had chased him away.

After a morning devoted to her daughter, Fran had a quick lunch and then drove over to leave Naomi with Jenny.

'What great news,' Jenny greeted her. 'You must feel wonderful.'

Fran hugged her daughter, before handing her over. 'I do. I'm over the moon. And that's a lie if ever I heard one,' she murmured to herself as she opened the front door.

'How's Callum?' Jenny asked.

'Fine.'

'Is he still at the cottage?'

'No. He was on duty early this morning.'

'I meant is he staying on there?'

'Not that I know of. Now the threat's gone there's no need, is there?'

'I don't know about that,' Jenny murmured suggestively.

I do, Fran thought, but she managed a coy smile of acknowledgement for Jenny.

Her heart raced as she completed the journey to the unit. Working with Cal in the future wasn't going to be easy. She was relieved that there was no sign of him when she arrived so she could concentrate on the hand-over.

'There's a problem with Mrs Dunn,' Kelly told her. 'She's not responding as Cal expected so he's gone to take another look at her blood cultures before he decides what to do.'

'She's still on IV antibiotics?'

Kelly nodded. 'Nothing's been changed since Friday. It's a pity Cal wasn't around this weekend. He nearly always pops in, even if it's his weekend off. He must have been away somewhere special this time. I'm sure he'd have acted sooner if he'd been here.'

Fran nodded noncommittally, hoping Kelly wouldn't notice the colour she knew was flooding into her cheeks. 'Any other problems?'

'Nothing urgent.' Kelly ran through the report on the remainder of the patients. 'The only thing outstanding is Mrs Lucas's discharge! Please!'

When the morning shift had left Fran did a quick round of the patients to update herself with their present condition. She could see what Kelly meant about Mrs Dunn. She was very much weaker than when Fran had last seen her on Friday. 'Is there anything I can get you?' she asked her patient gently.

Mrs Dunn shook her head and Fran checked her fluid balance chart.

'You haven't drunk much today,' she said. 'How about trying a little water or fruit juice now.'

Again the patient shook her head and closed her eyes. She seemed to have lost all interest in life over the weekend, and Fran prayed that Cal might find a clue in the blood cultures to stem her deterioration.

When she returned to the office she was surprised to find Cal there as she hadn't seen him arrive.

He looked up at her entrance and frowned. 'Something wrong?'

'I've just been talking to Mrs Dunn.'

He nodded. 'I'm going to change her antibiotics for these.' He had brought the drugs with him. 'Can you give me a hand with her infusion?'

Fran followed him into the ward, checked the present bag of fluid and went to get what he needed to change it.

When they had done so, and also arranged for Mrs Lucas to go home, Fran offered him a cup of tea. He accepted and followed her into the office. 'Everything OK when you left Naomi with Jenny?'

Fran nodded, but continued pouring the tea. 'Jenny seemed pleased that the threat has been lifted.'

'Aren't we all? It hasn't been an easy few days, has it?'

Fran looked up and surprised a wry quirk of his lips.

'It hasn't.' She handed him his tea, and ventured tentatively, 'I really am very grateful for all you've done for us.'

'But—B-U-T.' He spelled the letters out as he had the day before. '*But* you are now happier to return to your own company.'

She looked at him, aghast. 'That's unfair, Cal. I certainly didn't mean that.'

The telephone rang, preventing him from replying. He lifted the receiver and barked, 'Callum Smith.'

Although she tried not to eavesdrop, by updating her patients' records, Fran sensed he was being told something he wasn't happy about. The one-sided conversation went on for quite some time, and when he replaced the receiver, but left his hand resting on it without speaking, she asked, 'Problem?'

He shook his head. 'I can't believe it.' He closed the office door and cradled her in his arms. 'That was Jenny, Fran.'

'Yes?'

When he didn't answer she snapped, 'Cal. For goodness' sake tell me. What is it? Something wrong with Naomi?'

'Try to keep calm, Fran.'

'Cal? Is Naomi ill?'

He shook his head. 'She's been kidnapped.'

As Fran started to shriek hysterically he caught her to him and tried to comfort her. 'The police know and are already on the trail. She'll be back with Jenny soon.'

Tears were now gushing down Fran's cheeks. 'What happened, Cal? Is—was it someone connected with Dr Jenner?'

'The police think it was Jenner himself,' he told her quietly.

'But *surely* he's in custody?'

'He was released on bail at lunchtime.'

'Why on earth didn't they let us know?'

'Bad communications, love. When he eventually rustled up enough money they tried the cottage, and when you weren't there they made a note to try again later. I'm so sorry, love. I thought we'd covered all possibilities. They had the hospital number and my mobile number but they didn't try either. It was a policeman who hadn't been on duty over the weekend, and he didn't know there were other numbers to try.'

'I can't stay here, Cal. I'm going to look for her.' She started to open the office door.

He grasped her arm. 'There's nothing you can do at the moment, Fran, and you are needed here. The police know what they're doing.'

'That's rich,' she snapped. 'Did they know what they were doing when they didn't inform us he was out on bail?'

'Stay here, Fran, then I know where to contact you. I'm

off duty now so I'll go over to Jenny. She sounds in a terrible state and Brian is coming home from work.'

'Had Jenny left Naomi alone, Cal?'

'I don't know any details, Fran. They are not important. Getting her back is what matters now.'

Fran was sure he did know the details but was covering up for Jenny. She turned on him furiously. 'This is all your fault for making enquiries about Dr Jenner. If nothing had been done—'

'Fran!' She thought he was going to shake her, but he made a big effort to control himself. 'You know as well as I do that we couldn't ignore what was happening any longer.'

'But you said—you said last night—that Naomi was safe from now on.'

'I believed she was.' He cuddled her to him. 'I can't see what he hopes to gain...'

Fran suddenly realised that he was as distressed as she was. Had Naomi come to mean so much to him over the weekend? Could he care so much about another man's child?

Irritably, she dashed the irrational thought from her mind. They might never see Naomi again so what did it matter?

Cal released her and poured her another cup of tea. 'Drink this, Fran,' he said quietly, 'then get on with looking after your patients here. I promise no stone will be left unturned. Before I leave I'll tell Mrs Wood what's happening and I'll keep in touch with you here. When your shift finishes go to Jenny as normal.'

Fran watched him leave, wondering how he could be so calm. She knew he was right but she felt so helpless.

She must concentrate on her patients. That would help. She was completing the drug round when Mrs Wood came in search of her. 'How are you feeling now, Fran?'

'Dreadful.'

Mrs Wood waited until she had locked the drug trolley away, then said, 'I've asked the office to find cover for you. I think you'll feel better if you know what's going on.'

Fran felt tears welling in her eyes again. 'Thank you. Thank you so much. I—I just don't know what to do with myself.'

Mrs Wood smiled gently. 'I'm sure everything will turn out right. We're all praying for Naomi, Fran.'

Kelly joined them in the office at that moment and greeted Fran with a sympathetic smile. 'Well, I certainly didn't expect to be back here so soon. Any changes since I left?'

Fran gave her the details of the new regime of antibiotics for Mrs Dunn, and filled her in on a few other minor changes.

'Thanks, Kelly.'

She left the ward, watched sadly by Kelly and the consultant, and she knew they weren't as optimistic about Naomi's return as they'd made out.

She drove quickly to Jenny's house, then her fears returned with a vengeance as she realised that Naomi wasn't there, waiting for her, as usual.

Jenny opened the door before she could ring the bell. She enfolded Fran in her arms. 'I'm sorry, Fran. So sorry. It was all my fault. The telephone was ringing as I came through the door and I picked it up. If I'd still felt there was any threat I'd never have done it. I hardly turned my back for a moment because—it—there was no one there, and in that moment Naomi was snatched.'

'Has he been in contact?'

Jenny shook her head and led Fran through to where Brian and a policewoman were drinking tea.

'This is Anne.' Jenny introduced the officer. 'I'll get you some tea.' The whole time she spoke she was watching Fran as if she expected her to blow her top at any moment.

Fran took a deep breath and tried to remain calm. It was

not Jenny's fault and she mustn't let her think it was. She had problems enough of her own. Fran rested a hand on her friend's shoulder and muttered mechanically, 'I'm sure we'll soon have her back with us.'

After pacing the floor methodically for several minutes, she asked Anne dully, 'Is there anything at all I can do?'

The policewoman shook her head. 'It's best if you remain by the phone. Let us do the looking.'

'Where's Cal?' she asked, as Jenny handed her the tea.

Jenny shrugged and looked at Brian.

'He said he was going to follow up an idea of his own,' her husband volunteered.

They talked amongst themselves while Fran finished her tea, but she didn't hear a word of the conversation. She was too wrapped up in her own world of fear.

She suddenly felt she needed to be near Naomi's things. 'I—I think I'll go back to the cottage now,' she told them.

Jenny shook her head. 'You can't do that. We promised Cal we'd look after you here.'

Fran argued, but they all disagreed with her and eventually she capitulated.

It seemed dreadful, all of them sitting around there doing nothing. Trying to think about it rationally, Fran supposed that was all they could do. It wasn't fair to involve Jenny and Brian any further, and the policewoman was only doing her job. Unable to sit still, Fran paced the room repeatedly. Jenny tried to persuade her to eat something, but she couldn't do that either.

The telephone rang a couple of times, and Fran had to be restrained from snatching the receiver. Both times it was police colleagues to speak to Anne, but neither time had they any news.

When it was nearly midnight Jenny tried to persuade her to get some sleep. 'Anne will be here and will wake you the moment she hears anything.'

Fran had no intention of going to sleep until she knew

her baby was safe. 'I don't want to keep you two up, though. I can go back to the cottage.'

She was firmly told that wasn't an option. 'I'll go unless you two get some sleep,' she told them. 'I'll be all right. Anne's here with me.'

Despite protesting that there was no way they would be able to sleep, Jenny and Brian reluctantly agreed to go to bed. 'But only if you promise to wake us if anything happens,' Jenny insisted.

The night hours dragged for Fran. She heard Anne chattering, but didn't listen or respond. Her thoughts were solely for Naomi.

Where was she? How was she? Was she missing Fran? Was she frightened? The questions twisted repeatedly through her mind until it became a tangled mass of fear.

And where was Cal? He must know how frantic she would be by this time and yet there was not a word from him. Surely he could have at least rung.

As the night progressed she struggled to ignore increasingly sinister thoughts, but the thought that Naomi might be dead refused to be banished.

'There must be something we can do,' she muttered over and over, and she stared for long hours at the telephone, willing it to ring.

Each time Anne tried to reassure her. 'Leave it to those who know what they are doing. It's vitally important that you stay by the telephone. When they find Naomi she'll need you.'

'When, when, when,' Fran cried despondently. 'After all this time, surely you mean ''if''.'

CHAPTER TEN

ANNE placed a comforting arm around her. 'Don't, Fran. You mustn't give up hope. How about another cup of tea? Or coffee?'

Fran knew the policewoman was only trying to help but her irritation overflowed at the offer. The first streaks of dawn were showing in the sky, and her self-control snapped. 'I don't want anything. I just want to give Naomi her breakfast.'

Although tears had never been far from her eyes, sobs now racked her body with a despair she couldn't control.

Anne hugged Fran to her. 'Calm down, love. You've done so well up to now. Why don't you try and get some sleep?'

'Sleep?' Fran hiccoughed hysterically. 'Could you sleep, knowing you've lost the one person you love?'

'You haven't lost her, Fran. I'm sure she'll be back safe and sound with you soon.'

'It's easy for you to say that.' Fran sniffed hopelessly, before adding, 'I'm sorry, Anne. I know you're only trying to help.'

'I understand, love. And, whatever you say, I'm going to make us another cup of tea.'

Fran nodded and subsided into her chair. 'I just feel so helpless. And hopeless. I want to scream and scream, but I know it won't help. Oh, Anne. What can I do? How will I ever live without her? Help me... Help me...' Her sobs returned with such force that she couldn't continue.

Anne tried hopelessly to comfort her, but no longer tried to reassure her that all was well, and Fran guessed this was because she, too, had lost hope as the hours had passed.

Paradoxically, Fran felt the need to reassure the police-woman, to let her know she'd done her best and that Fran appreciated it and certainly didn't blame her.

The kettle had just boiled when the front doorbell pealed, making Fran jump. She was way ahead in the race to the front door, with the policewoman close behind in case she was needed.

As Fran struggled to open the door she heard Jenny's loud whisper from the stairs. 'What's happening?'

Neither bothered to answer. Fran was frantically trying to release the chain with shaking hands, and Anne was anxious to protect Fran from any danger and also determined not to miss a detail of any event that she might have to describe in evidence.

Fran eventually managed to tug the door open and, despite the late hour, she couldn't contain an excited yelp.

Cal was standing there, flanked by two policemen, but, most important of all, he was cuddling a blanketed bundle to his chest.

'Naomi,' Fran shrieked as she scrabbled at the blanket, attempting to identify the contents. 'It *is* Naomi, isn't it? Isn't it, Cal?' Her voice was rising uncontrollably.

He smiled and wordlessly handed over his charge. Fran pulled the blanket right away.

'It is. It is Naomi!' She turned towards the policewoman and displayed her daughter, in her excitement totally forgetting that Anne wouldn't recognise the child.

'Could we come in now?' a smiling Cal asked. 'It is a little parky out here.'

Suddenly realising that she was blocking the doorway, Fran moved away as if in a trance. Cal followed close behind and the three police officers brought up the rear, conversing in undertones.

Jenny and Brian excitedly joined them in the back room, oblivious of their attire. Brian was wearing tartan pyjama bottoms and Jenny the matching top, with black bikini briefs peeping out below.

They checked for themselves that it really was Naomi. Fran stood in the middle of the room, ecstatically crooning to her daughter, tears of joy streaming down her cheeks. She didn't realise how dangerously she was swaying until Cal and one of the policemen grabbed her.

Anne quickly moved an armchair up behind her and, encircling her with his arms, Cal gently guided her into it. He knelt beside her and murmured, 'She's not hurt, Fran, I promise you. I checked and she's fine. Let me tell you exactly what happened and—'

'Not now.' Fran didn't want to hear any details—only to cuddle her baby and check for herself that she hadn't been harmed. In any way. 'Has she been fed?'

'Last night. She certainly doesn't seem hungry at the moment.'

'But—but she's all right, is she? She hasn't been drugged or anything like—?'

'I'm sure she hasn't. She was wide awake when we found her and by that time ''Dr Jenner'' was prepared to tell us exactly what he'd done. I can assure you, this is natural sleep.'

She dragged her eyes away from Naomi and met his gaze for the first time. 'It w-was you who found her?'

Clearly pleased with himself, he nodded.

Fran shook her head, trying to shake off the muzzy effects of exhaustion which were preventing her from thinking clearly.

'Where?' she managed to ask.

He grinned. 'You'll never guess. I can see a whole new career as a detective opening up for me!'

Ignoring him, Fran persisted, 'Where was she, Cal?'

'Mrs Dubarry's empty house! I outsmarted your ''Dr Jenner''. He didn't know I knew about that.'

Fran shuddered violently. 'He's not *my* ''Dr Jenner''.'

Her shudder progressed into a continuous shiver and what little colour she had had in her cheeks drained away.

Jenny, who had been listening with disbelief, took one of Fran's hands in her own. 'She's frozen.'

With one arm around her shoulders, Cal had already turned to Brian. 'Blankets, quick. It's a touch of delayed shock.'

As Fran closed her eyes and rested her head back on Cal's arm, Jenny attempted to take Naomi, but Fran grasped her daughter even more firmly.

Cal moved to try and release her hold. 'It's all right now, Fran,' he cajoled quietly. 'Naomi's safe here. Let Jenny take her for a moment while we cover you up with a blanket.'

But Fran held her close. 'No-o. I must keep her with me.'

Biting her bottom lip, Jenny looked up at Cal. 'She blames me, doesn't she?'

'Of course not, Jenny. She's just overwrought. I think it'll be best if I take them both back to the cottage and Fran gets some sleep. If that's OK by everyone.'

'We need to talk to you both,' one of the policemen said to him, 'but it can wait until later in the morning.'

Cal nodded. 'Come on, Fran. We're going home.' He raised her from the chair and wrapped her in another blanket. 'OK if we let you have these back tomorrow?'

Jenny hastily agreed. 'No problem. We don't use them.'

Fran suddenly pulled back. 'We can't go to the cottage. Dr Jenner—he might be there.'

Cal's arm tightened reassuringly round her shoulder as the older policeman smiled. 'I certainly hope not. By now he should be safely tucked up in a hospital secure unit.'

'But—but you let him go last time or this wouldn't have happened. How do we know he won't just walk out of the hospital?' Fran asked accusingly.

'Because it's a secure unit and because he realises the

game is up. He's blown his insurance, in other words, and you're no longer a threat to him,' Cal broke in. 'Come on. I'm taking you and Naomi home. Give me your car keys.'

Still bewildered, Fran did as he asked.

'Would you like us to bring your car over to the cottage later, sir?' a policeman asked.

'I'd appreciate that,' Cal told him.

Fran looked at him anxiously. 'Why? Where is it? Has something happened—?'

'Stop expecting the worst, Fran,' Cal broke in. 'I couldn't drive *and* hold Naomi, could I?'

'But the policeman could have held her.'

He smiled again. 'No way. I wanted to hand Naomi over to you personally, and had no intention of relinquishing my charge to anyone.'

'You mean you abandoned your precious BMW for Naomi?'

'And for you,' he told her softly as he helped her into the back seat of her own car, before leaning over and kissing her gently on the lips. In her exhausted state Fran started to cry softly. But this time with joy.

'I—I—don't know how I'll ever be able to thank you, Cal.'

'We'll find a way, don't you worry,' he said with a confident smile as he slid behind the steering-wheel of her car.

His words sent a shiver of cautious optimism down the length of her spine. Was finding Naomi safe and sound a turning point in her life? Could she trust Cal?

Throughout the journey to the cottage she tried unsuccessfully to think positively. She wanted to believe that this time it could be different. Especially after he'd rescued Naomi for her. Perhaps it would have helped if she'd listened when he'd tried to tell her exactly what had happened and how he had found her, but she was so tired and her emotions so tightly strung that she found it difficult to think rationally.

When they arrived at the cottage he said, 'Stay there while I unlock the door.'

Too tired to argue, she did as he ordered, but when he tried to take Naomi from her arms she clung to her tightly. 'I can manage.'

She cringed inside as she saw his left eyebrow lift with hurt resignation. She felt guilty at her refusal, but after all that had happened she still wasn't ready to relinquish control.

Once indoors Naomi started to cry. Fran checked her watch and shook her head. 'I can't believe this. It's her usual waking time.'

'Can I get you anything?'

Fran was hesitant. 'I—I'd like to bath and change Naomi before I get her breakfast.'

Cal nodded understandingly. 'Can I get *you* a cup of something?'

Fran laughed as she shook her head. 'I'm already water-logged. Anne drip-fed me liquids throughout the night, even when I didn't want them.'

She carried Naomi up the stairs and into the bathroom, where she undressed her and then examined her from head to toe. Whatever Cal had said, she had to check for herself that every inch of her daughter was unharmed.

Naomi splashed happily in her bath for a short time, but then remembered she was hungry and started to bawl again.

Fran heard Cal come up the stairs. 'Can I come in?'

'Do—but we won't be long. Naomi's empty tummy won't wait.'

'Her breakfast's all ready,' he told her quietly.

She gave him a grateful look. 'Thanks, Cal.'

'While you feed her I'll get you some breakfast. Eggs and bacon all right?'

She shook her head. 'I—I couldn't eat a thing.'

'Oh, yes, you could. And you will. I'm not having you faint at my feet again,' he teased.

By the time Naomi had been fed Cal had prepared an enormous breakfast for them both. 'I found mushrooms and tomatoes in the fridge. Hope it was OK to use them.'

She nodded. 'But I'm not sure I can eat all that.'

He smiled. 'You will.'

Although she felt too tired to eat, once she started on the food Fran realised how hungry she was and ate it with appreciation. By the time she was replete she felt much better. Even some of her tiredness had lifted.

She checked that Naomi was playing happily in her carry seat, then settled back with a second cup of coffee and said, 'Now, tell me exactly what happened.'

'Aren't you tired? I can watch Naomi while you have a kip.'

'I won't be able to sleep until I know everything. Unless *you* need to sleep?' she added, suddenly concerned that she didn't know exactly what he'd been through.

He shook his head. 'But let's move to a more comfortable seat. And, before I start, I must ring the unit to let them know we won't be in to work today—not that they'll expect us!'

Having done that, he settled beside her on the settee and placed an arm gently around her.

'When I left Jenny and Brian I went to Mrs Dubarry's old house.'

Fran nodded.

'I didn't want to barge straight in in case I was right, about Naomi being there. Our man might have panicked if I did, so I peered through the windows.

'After a time I could hear a baby crying and I saw a man, pacing up and down with her in his arms. I guessed he must be the bogus doctor. Unless he had an accomplice. Whoever he was, at least he appeared to be taking care of her so, not wanting to antagonise him, I crept away and used my mobile phone to alert the police.

'When they arrived they said they were worried about

what might happen if they tried to force an entrance. Apparently, they'd discovered he was thrown out of medical school because, although he had a good brain, he had an inadequate personality.'

Fran gasped loudly, and Cal hugged her tightly. 'Nothing did happen, Fran, I promise, because I watched everything that went on from the back of a police car. While the police and a psychiatrist they had managed to rustle up tried to negotiate through the closed front door, another team of policemen were attempting to prise open the patio door.

'They had to do it carefully as they didn't want to make a noise or rush him, for Naomi's sake. He cradled her in his arms throughout.'

Fran bit on her curled index finger to prevent herself crying out.

'When he realised he was surrounded he just collapsed into a heap, and one of the policewomen took Naomi from him. It was all over so quickly it was unbelievable.'

'But—but why did it take so long to let us know—?'

'It's quick in the telling, but it took time for the police to arrive and to get into position and to contact the psychiatrist. Then they were negotiating with him for a long time.'

Her cheeks wet with tears, Fran searched for and held Cal's gaze with eyes full of admiration. 'I have so much to thank you for. I owe you so very, very, much.'

Reaching up, she gently pulled his head towards her so that their lips met.

She had intended it to be a chaste kiss of gratitude, nothing more, but he held her close, and his warm lips snatched the initiative, pressing against hers with a gentle firmness that wouldn't allow her to draw away.

Not that she tried. Her breathing deepened and her lips parted to allow the slow invasion of his tongue, searching and probing by teasing stages so that all reason was replaced by an overwhelming sensation of helplessness that she didn't want to end.

When they eventually drew apart, the loss she felt was so acute that it took a deep breath to steady her before she could meet his eyes again. When she did, she found he was smiling down at her with such an expression of tenderness that her yearning senses hoped for more, much more. When he eventually loosened his hold the tears his kiss had stemmed started to stream down her cheeks again.

He took her head between his hands and gently wiped away the tears with his thumbs. 'Fran,' he whispered, but his words were drowned by Naomi, emitting a loud grizzle at being ignored.

Fran crossed the room and lifted her into her arms. 'Another dirty nappy,' she told Cal with a resigned smile. 'I'll change it and then she'll probably be ready for a nap.'

As she left the room she thought she heard him say, 'You and me, too.' She wished she felt the same, but there was so much she still wanted to know. About the bogus doctor, about Cal and especially where she and Cal went from here.

When Naomi had settled, Fran rejoined Cal in the living room, and saw that the breakfast dishes had been cleared, washed and put away. He was lounging on the settee and patted the cushion beside him.

'Come and sit down for a moment.'

'Thanks for clearing away.'

He dismissed her thanks with an airy wave of his hand. 'Fran, I think we both need to catch up on our sleep, but before we do I want to clarify a few things.'

Fran was immediately apprehensive. 'Such as?'

'Such as our future, hopefully together.'

'There's nothing I'd like better, Cal—'

'B-U-T?' he challenged.

She hesitated, before deciding she had to air her doubts. 'I know you've told me you're not married, but—'

He sighed. 'I guess I should have told you about Marcia long ago.'

He must have read the dismay in her face. 'It was all over before I came to Wenton, Fran, but I was still hurting and didn't want to talk about it.'

'Tell me about her,' she murmured, running her hand encouragingly up and down his arm.

He thought for a moment. 'We lived together for three years. She was a model. When I accepted this job I thought it would be the opportunity to get married and start a family. She used to talk about other men, but I thought they were the people she worked with.'

'And?'

'One night when I was on call she skedaddled off to London with one of them, leaving a note. I should have realised long before, but I was too busy with my work.'

'I—'

He put a finger to her lips to still her interruption.

'Now you know why I was so suspicious of you and Rob. In the beginning I thought you were cheating on Naomi's father.'

Fran shook her head in disbelief, and with a wry smile he replaced his finger with his lips. 'I'm sorry,' he breathed, 'but Marcia had sapped my trust in the opposite sex.

'She said that her modelling career was far too important for her to spoil her figure with childbirth or to move to a backwater like Wenton. I suppose in the end I was just miffed that she thought so little of me that she couldn't even discuss it face to face. My pride was probably more hurt than anything.

'I moved to Wenton and threw myself wholeheartedly into my work. Then I met you. I thought you had everything I'd always wanted. Until Jenny told me your husband was dead.

'I knew immediately that I wanted to take his place— that was why I wangled you an invitation to the firm dinner—but I soon discovered you were still grieving over Daniel and I realised that I would have to give it time.'

Fran gasped. Was it just a family he was searching for? The last thing she needed was someone who loved Naomi and not her mother. 'What are you trying to say?'

'Just that I want to marry you and take care of you both for the rest of your lives.'

She smiled and kissed him on the cheek. 'It's a very tempting offer, Cal, but I'm not sure I can accept.'

He frowned. 'I know it's been a difficult time for you and, as you said on Sunday night, we were thrown together in a very artificial situation. That's why I thought it would be better if I moved out.

'I intended to give us both a breathing space so that next time I tried to find the key to your heart it would be under normal conditions. But Jenner put paid to that, by snatching Naomi.'

Fran frowned thoughtfully. 'I'm very grateful for everything you've done for us, Cal, but if you're just looking for a ready-made family it—'

He lifted his index finger to her lips to silence her protest. 'I hear what you're trying to say, Fran. I just want you and Naomi to be happy. If the only way you will be is for me to butt out of your lives completely, I'm quite prepared to do that.'

Fran's heart plummeted at the suggestion.

'But I certainly don't want to.' He took her in his arms. 'Is there a problem, Fran?'

She didn't answer immediately, and while he waited his lips sought hers, gently at first but then, as if to impress her with his sincerity, with a firmness she found impossible to resist. Her breathing quickened and a helplessness overwhelmed her, making all rational thought impossible.

'Tell me, Fran. Please?' he murmured softly. 'Will you let me take care of you both permanently?'

Take care. Not love. Take care of, but he didn't love her.

Her thoughts were bleak as she struggled to overcome her desire for him. However she had hurt him, he must still love Marcia.

'It wouldn't work, Cal. It would be a mistake. For both of us.'

The pain and misery her words etched on his face spelt the death knell to her dreams.

'It wouldn't be a mistake for either of us if you loved me even half as much as I love you.' His voice was anguished and he pulled her close to his body, trailing kisses down her cheek and across her neck as he murmured into her hair, 'I love you so much, Fran.'

Relief swept through her. 'Why didn't you say so earlier? I really believed that it was Naomi who was the main attraction.'

'Did you honestly think I would have slept with you if I didn't love you?'

'Oh, Cal. What a fool I've been. After Daniel I suppose I found it difficult—'

Her words were smothered by his lips caressing hers in a kiss that was slow and deep.

She sighed, and her hands moved slowly across his broad back. He groaned and slowly trailed his finger over her shoulder until he found the hardened peak of her breast.

She gasped with pleasure.

'Let's go to bed before Naomi wakes,' he whispered.

The remainder of the day was disjointed. While Naomi slept they made love and slept themselves. When she was awake they shared her care. In between, two policemen arrived with Cal's car and to take their statements.

'Was ''Dr Jenner'' completely bogus?' Fran asked before they began.

'Unfortunately. He started training at medical school but was thrown out in the second year. He used his brother's name and qualifications so that if anyone checked he wouldn't be found out.'

'Didn't his brother know?'

'He's working abroad and had no idea. When our Dr Jenner realised the G.M.C. were involved he panicked at the thought of his brother being struck off, and thought if he kidnapped Naomi he could prevent it happening.'

'Poor chap, he's more to be pitied than reviled. His brother was always the one who'd got him out of scrapes and he was terrified of what he'd started.'

'What did he intend doing with Naomi?'

'I don't think he knew. He just saw her as his insurance policy. One thing in his favour. When we questioned him he was anxious to know that she was back safely with you. I don't believe he intended her any harm.'

When the policemen eventually left, Fran said, 'I should have rung Jenny long ago. She must be frantic by this time.'

'Why don't you go and visit her? I have a couple of things to do at the shops so I'll drop you and Naomi there for a short time.'

Jenny was delighted to see her. 'Are you going to work?'

Fran shook her head. 'Not until the early shift tomorrow. Will that be all right?'

'Of course. Anytime. It means you've forgiven me.'

'Forgiven you? For what? It was all my fault for not telling you the whole truth. I'm so sorry, Jen. But let's put all that behind us. I have some more exciting news. You were right about Cal. He does have a thing about me! And Naomi.'

'Great, Fran. I'm so happy for you.'

Cal collected them later than he had promised, but on the way back to the cottage he refused to tell Fran why he was late or where he had been.

They shared Naomi's bedtime routine and when she eventually settled, Cal produced another gourmet spread from his favourite convenience counter.

'But before we eat—an appetiser.' He produced a bottle

of dry champagne. Before opening it, he sank onto one knee and said, 'Will you marry me, Fran? As soon as it can be arranged?'

When she nodded breathlessly, he took her left hand in his own and slid a ring onto her finger.

'Cal. It's beautiful. Diamonds and sapphires. It's what I would have chosen myself. How did you know?'

'I didn't know, but I guessed. I'm pleased I got it right.'

She waved her beringed hand towards the table and the champagne and the red wine. 'I can't take all this, Cal.'

'You're not taking anything because I'm giving. All I need is for you to tell me regularly how much you love me.'

'I love you, Cal. More than I can ever put into words.'

'Hopefully, we've both found the loving family we've missed out on so far.'

Fran clapped her hand to her mouth. 'I'd forgotten. Mum and Dad are due home tomorrow and they don't even know about Naomi yet, never mind you.'

He grinned. 'It's probably easier to get all the shocks over in one go! Especially when we're giving them something to celebrate. In the meantime, let's make the most of tonight on our own.'

Jenny was delighted to hear Fran's news when she dropped Naomi off the next morning. 'Congratulations! If there's anything I can do to help, just let me know.'

The news appeared to have preceded her arrival for the early shift and everyone congratulated her. 'Not that we're not green-eyed,' Michelle told her, 'but we do hope you'll both be very happy.'

Fran was pleased when she learnt from the hand-over report that Mrs Dunn was responding to the new antibiotics. 'Cal popped in yesterday to check and he was delighted with her progress.' So that was where he'd been.

Cal was in Outpatients for the morning and when the

clinic finished he and Mrs Wood came in search of Fran. 'I'm delighted, dear. The best thing that could have happened. For you both.'

Over coffee Cal said, 'We've an admission this afternoon. Mrs Fenner is coming back with her diabetes hopelessly out of control.'

'You expected that, didn't you? I remember your pessimism when you discharged her. Until then I thought your glass was always half-full,' she teased.

He closed the door and said quietly, 'I do have a reason for that. My sister was a diabetic and my father never accepted the fact. He said Mum was making a ridiculous fuss, and while Mum was in hospital, having me, he left Katy with a child-minder, without telling her that she must ensure Katy ate her meal after having her dose of insulin. Katy died that night. Mum never got over it, and I suppose Dad never forgave himself, although he never admitted it.'

'Cal! How dreadful.'

He shrugged. 'It was all a long time ago, but whenever I come across a relative like Mr Fenner it reminds me that, but for Dad, I might have had a sister.'

'Was that why I sensed you didn't approve of child-minders as well?'

He nodded. 'More than likely. But Jenny's your friend. That's the difference.'

'So you won't object if once we're married I leave Naomi with her and come to work?'

'I don't know about that. I think I've said more than once that I see you as a home-maker first and a career girl second.'

'But you wouldn't mind if I worked part time?'

'As long as Jenny is the child-minder. I won't have my children looked after by strangers.'

'Your children?'

'At least four. We don't want to run the risk of Naomi having no family to turn to in the future.'

'True,' Fran conceded.

'Another B-U-T?'

'Not really. I was just wondering how soon you were envisaging this football team.'

'How about asking Jenny to keep Naomi this afternoon and I'll sneak off for a couple of hours? Then we could make a start.'

'Callum Smith, how could you suggest such a thing? I still haven't caught up on my sleep.'

'You'll sleep better with me by your side.'

'I'm not sure how to take that,' she teased. 'I don't want Mum and Dad to find me worn out!'

'Talking of worn out, you remember Miss George who I handed over to the rheumatologists?'

'The lady with the severe headaches?'

'That's the one. She came to Outpatients earlier and when they'd confirmed how well she is doing on the tablets she came in search of me. To thank me for my magic. And do you know what she told me? She's moving so well she's taken up line dancing. At eighty-three! She showed me a photograph!'

'Are you suggesting I should do the same?'

'Far from it. I was just pointing out that as I can obviously work miracles a couple of hours in bed with me will rejuvenate you.'

That evening her mother rang from the nearby hotel where Fran had booked a room for them.

'I can't get over there tonight, Mum, but I'm desperate to see you. I'll organise a taxi to bring you here.'

'Aren't you well, Fran?'

'I've never felt better.' Not giving her a chance to argue, she added, 'I'll see you soon.' Then she cut the call.

She rushed to the door the moment she heard the taxi she'd ordered turn into the drive. 'It's wonderful to see you,' she told her parents as she kissed them both. 'Come through to the kitchen. I'm sorry I couldn't come to the hotel, but I have a surprise for you.'

She opened the door to reveal Cal, feeding Naomi. 'This is Dr Smith, Mum, Callum Smith. And this is Naomi.'

Her mother's jaw dropped as she looked pointedly at the engagement ring alone on Fran's finger. 'You—you're not married?'

'Dada-dada,' Naomi chanted, delighted by all the attention.

'We were waiting for you to come home for that.' Cal placated her hurriedly. 'Fran told me that, as your only daughter, she wanted you to be there.'

'It's a pity you couldn't wait to start your family as well,' Fran's mother admonished Callum tartly.

'Yes. Well, Naomi isn't—' he started to explain, but Fran silenced him.

'Cal has no living relatives, Mum. Having a daughter is the best thing that could have happened to him.'

Fran smiled sweetly at them each in turn. 'If you come upstairs with me, Mum, you can help me bath her and I'll tell you all about it. Cal can find Dad a drink.'

She looked at her bemused father and winked at Cal. He opened his eyes wide and Fran knew she was in for trouble later—but it would be the kind of trouble she enjoyed!

In the meantime, she would tell her mother the truth and, hopefully, Cal would do the same for her father.

When her parents finally left to return to their hotel for the night, their heads buzzing with imminent wedding plans for their only child, Fran locked the door behind them and moved into Cal's arms.

He held her close and murmured, 'I do love you so very, very, much, Fran. When you introduced Naomi as my daughter it was the proudest moment of my life. Thank you, thank you, my darling.'

'She's the first, Cal. It won't be long until more little Smiths join her.'

As she spoke she watched a look of soft tenderness spread across his face, and laughed with delight when he said, 'At last. Your glass is half-full!'

MILLS & BOON®

*M*akes
any time special

Enjoy a romantic novel from
Mills & Boon®

Presents™ *Enchanted*™ *Temptation*

Historical Romance™ *Medical Romance*™

MILLS & BOON®

Medical Romance™

COMING NEXT MONTH

All these books are especially for Mother's Day

✳   ✳   ✳

A HERO FOR MOMMY by Jessica Matthews

Dr Ben Shepherd was unprepared for the impact Kelly Evers and her five-year-old daughter Carlie would have on his life...

BE MY MUMMY by Josie Metcalfe

Jack Madison's small son Danny was a delight, and he and Lauren were very drawn to each other. But why does this make Jack edgy?

MUM'S THE WORD by Alison Roberts

Dr Sarah Kendall anticipated a happy family life when she accepted Paul's proposal, but Paul's son Daniel had other ideas!

WANTED: A MOTHER by Elisabeth Scott

Adam Kerr needed a live-in nurse for his ten-year-old daughter Jeannie, but Meg Bennett was *so* much younger and prettier than he expected...

Available from 5th March 1999

Available at most branches of WH Smith, Tesco, Asda,
Martins, Borders, Easons, Volume One/James Thin
and most good paperback bookshops

MILLS & BOON®

Next Month's Romance Titles

♡

Each month you can choose from a wide variety of romance novels from Mills & Boon®. Below are the new titles to look out for next month from the Presents™ and Enchanted™ series.

Presents™

THE MARRIAGE DECIDER	Emma Darcy
TO BE A BRIDEGROOM	Carole Mortimer
HOT SURRENDER	Charlotte Lamb
THE BABY SECRET	Helen Brooks
A HUSBAND'S VENDETTA	Sara Wood
BABY DOWN UNDER	Ann Charlton
A RECKLESS SEDUCTION	Jayne Bauling
OCCUPATION: MILLIONAIRE	Alexandra Sellers

Enchanted™

A WEDDING WORTH WAITING FOR	Jessica Steele
CAROLINE'S CHILD	Debbie Macomber
SLEEPLESS NIGHTS	Anne Weale
ONE BRIDE DELIVERED	Jeanne Allan
A FUNNY THING HAPPENED...	Caroline Anderson
HAND-PICKED HUSBAND	Heather MacAllister
A MOST DETERMINED BACHELOR	Miriam Macgregor
INTRODUCING DADDY	Alaina Hawthorne

On sale from 5th March 1999

H1 9902

Available at most branches of WH Smith, Tesco, Asda, Martins, Borders, Easons, Volume One/James Thin and most good paperback bookshops

MILLS & BOON®

Makes any time special™

By Request

Bestselling themed romances brought back to you by popular demand

Each month By Request brings you three full–length novels in one beautiful volume featuring the best of the best.

So if you missed a favourite Romance the first time around, here is your chance to relive the magic from some of our most popular authors.

Look out for
Conveniently Yours **in February 1999 featuring Emma Darcy, Helen Bianchin and Michelle Reid**

Available at most branches of WH Smith, Tesco, Asda, Martins, Borders, Easons, Volume One/James Thin and most good paperback bookshops

MILLS & BOON®

Makes any time special™

By Request

Bestselling themed romances brought back to you by popular demand

Each month By Request brings you three
full-length novels in one beautiful volume
featuring the best of the best.

So if you missed a favourite Romance
the first time around, here is your chance
to relive the magic from some of our
most popular authors.

Look out for
***Sole Paternity* in March 1999**
featuring Miranda Lee, Robyn Donald
and Sandra Marton

Available at most branches of WH Smith, Tesco,
Asda, Martins, Borders, Easons,
Volume One/James Thin
and most good paperback bookshops

FREE!

2 Books
and a surprise gift!

We would like to take this opportunity to thank you for reading this Mills & Boon® book by offering you the chance to take TWO more specially selected titles from the Medical Romance™ series absolutely FREE! We're also making this offer to introduce you to the benefits of the Reader Service™—

- ★ FREE home delivery
- ★ FREE gifts and competitions
- ★ FREE monthly Newsletter
- ★ Books available before they're in the shops
- ★ Exclusive Reader Service discounts

Accepting these FREE books and gift places you under no obligation to buy; you may cancel at any time, even after receiving your free shipment. Simply complete your details below and return the entire page to the address below. *You don't even need a stamp!*

YES! Please send me 2 free Medical Romance books and a surprise gift. I understand that unless you hear from me, I will receive 4 superb new titles every month for just £2.40 each, postage and packing free. I am under no obligation to purchase any books and may cancel my subscription at any time. The free books and gift will be mine to keep in any case.

M9EB

Ms/Mrs/Miss/Mr ....Initials..
BLOCK CAPITALS PLEASE

Surname..

Address..

....

....Postcode ....

Send this whole page to:
THE READER SERVICE, FREEPOST CN81, CROYDON, CR9 3WZ
(Eire readers please send coupon to: P.O. Box 4546, Dublin 24.)

DIANA PALMER

ONCE in PARIS

Brianne Martin rescued grief-stricken Pierce
Hutton from the depths of despair, but before
she knew it, Brianne had become a pawn in an
international web of deceit and corruption.
Now it was Pierce's turn to rescue Brianne.
What had they stumbled into?
They would be lucky to escape with their lives!

1-55166-470-4
MIRA® Available in paperback from March, 1999